BAD BLOWS

THE WINSTON BROTHERS
BOOK FOUR

DORI PULITANO

Cover designed by Taylored Designs
Editor: Sandy Ebel, Personal Touch Editing

Author Dori Pulitano

Ryker

THE SOUNDS of flesh hitting flesh and the scent of sweat and blood fill the space. My eyes are riveted to the young men going toe to toe inside the twenty-by-twenty ring. The time counts down as they draw closer to the buzzer, and my bet is on the newest member of my club, Axel. He's barely eighteen years old but shows tons of potential. Hell, at his size, he could be the next superstar. At six feet, his muscular build makes him a perfect opponent. He walked in the front door of Strykers, my boxing gym, and I knew he would fit in perfectly with the rest of us.

I built the gym about a year ago, right after I got out of prison and lost everything. My career was flushed down the drain when I got caught up in something I had no business being involved in—something that inevitably ruined me. No longer the 'Saint' of boxing, I now use my skills to coach men who want to be turned into something more.

"That's it, Axel. Hit him with an uppercut," I holler as Axel throws his final punch, taking his equally formidable opponent to the ground. "Meet me in the office."

I turn from the fight and head toward the back, where my private office is. Passing the counter, Christy, the front desk receptionist, catches my eye and smiles. She's been laying it on thick the last few days, making her interest in me known.

"That girl wants your dick bad, boss." Luke chuckles as he meets me in the hallway. "You gonna tap it or what?"

Glancing back over my shoulder, I spot her eyeing me as I step through my office door. "Yeah… not going to happen. I need a woman, not a girl."

"Pussy is pussy, boss." Luke drops into the chair opposite mine. "And it's well past the time for you to dip your wick in some ink, if you know what I mean." He waggles his eyebrows, making me roll my eyes.

Grunting at his absurd suggestion, I drop into my chair and sigh. "Thanks, but I'll pass. Maybe you should fuck her. She seems like your type, anyway."

Luke leans his head back and laughs. "Maybe I will."

A knock at the door halts our banter. "Come in."

Axel steps through the door and pauses. "You wanted to see me?"

"I did. Have a seat." I wave to the empty chair beside Luke. "I have news. It appears there's going to be an armature fight in a few weeks, and I'd like for you to represent Strykers."

Axel glances between Luke and me. "You serious?"

"Yeah, kid. I'm serious. You've been pushing yourself hard, and I think you're ready."

"I don't know, man." Axel leans forward, pressing his elbows into his knees. "This is a pretty big deal. I don't want to embarrass you or your brand. You sure I'm the right fighter?"

"I think you're the perfect choice." Sitting up in my chair, I rest my forearms on my desk. "You remind me of me."

"What about you? Why don't you fight?"

Closing my eyes, I take a deep breath and sigh. "I'm not sure I'll ever step into the ring again."

"Bullshit." This time, it's Luke who speaks. "You need to get back in the ring at some point, Ryker. You can't hide out forever. The Saint deserves a rebirth."

I shake my head. "I think my time has come and gone."

Axel looks over at Luke and smirks. "I'll do it on one condition."

Leaning back, I fold my arms across my chest and narrow my gaze on the cocky shit smirking at me.

"And that is what, exactly?"

"I'll do it if you train me. Get in the ring and show me how to win the way you did."

My gaze travels between the two men sitting in front of me, and I can't help but laugh.

"You told him already, didn't you?"

"Maybe I did." Luke shrugs. "I figured if you got back in there, you'd see what you were missing. What happened was bullshit, and you paid too high of a price."

"Are you referring to prison or nearly dying?" My fingers instinctively seek the scar beneath my shirt. The three-inch raised skin is my reminder of what I nearly lost. "This is dirty… even for you."

Luke laughs as he glances toward Axel. "You sure you're ready for the 'Saint'? He won't go easy on you if he agrees to do this."

"If he agrees, it'll be worth every bruise."

"You're speaking as if I'm not even in the room." I toss a pen at Luke's head, then look at Axel. "If I agree with this, you'll do everything I say. Follow every order and show up at the times I dictate."

"Hell, Ryker, I'd wash your fucking truck every day for a year if *you* agree to train me."

Watching Axel as my mind mulls over working with him and the possibilities it will bring for him… and me, I sigh.

"Fine. You've got yourself a deal. Meet me here tomorrow night at seven p.m. We're going to hit it hard, Axel. This won't be like the baby shit you've been doing in the ring. Training is going to be twice as hard and three times as long. Nothing can come before this, you understand?"

"Yeah, I got you, Ryker." Axel stands and extends his hand. "Thank you for taking a chance on me. I won't let you down."

"Let's hope I don't let you down."

Axel steps out of the office, leaving me and Luke alone.

"You're a twat." I cut my eyes to my best friend. "This was a setup."

"Yep. I won't deny it, either. You need a push, Ryker. What happened a year ago was bullshit, and you know it. That mother fucker set you up, then tried to take you out inside the joint."

"Doesn't matter… he won, and I lost—everything."

"You didn't lose everything." Luke pushes to his feet and starts toward the door. "It was merely a setback, Ryk. It's up to you to make a comeback or not. Either way, I'm with you, whatever you decide. You feel like sparring?"

"Right now?"

"No time like the present. It's like riding a bike… you just need to get back on."

A laugh slips past my lips. "Fine. I'll meet you in the ring in thirty. I need to do the budget and pay some bills, or we won't have a ring to spar in."

"Yeah, yeah."

Luke shuts me inside the room, and I lean back in my seat, closing my eyes. I miss the thrill of the crowd, but fear keeps me from getting back inside the ring. My mind drifts back to the night my life changed forever.

"What do you mean he's going to fight dirty?" I glance at my trainer in question. "The refs won't allow it. He'll be kicked out, and I'll win by a technicality."

"We believe he's going to come at you before you even step into the ring, Ryker."

I close my eyes and sigh. "This is complete bullshit. Is he that much of a pussy that he plans to fuck with me outside of the arena?"

"We don't know. Which is why we think you should postpone the fight."

"No. I'm not giving in to this jackass. I'm fighting tonight. Come hell or high water."

The sound of the phone ringing jerks me from my thoughts. Snatching the device from my desk, I glance at the screen. *Unknown*

Number flashes across the screen. This is the third time it's rung with an unknown number displaying. Groaning, I press the speaker button and speak.

"Ryker Nash."

"Um... Mr. Nash?" The sweetest voice I've ever heard blasts through the tiny speaker of my phone, socking me square in the gut.

"That's what I said." I stare down at the phone. "Can I help you with something?"

"I..." the woman pauses. "My name is Miss Quincy... I represent the law firm—"

"I'm not interested in whatever you're trying to get," I cut her off before she can finish her words. "I told the last three bloodsucking attorneys who called I have no desire to sue anyone."

Hitting the end button, I drop my phone onto the desk and sigh. After I was released from prison, ambulance chasers came out of the woodwork to get me to sue the state penitentiary. They were convinced I'd win a lawsuit because they'd placed me in danger, putting me in the general population. Seeing I was a nationally renowned boxer—one who'd ended the life of a well-known thug wanna-be—I had a target on my back the minute I stepped into prison to serve my one-year sentence. Being shanked in the court-yard sped my release up. Guess they figured my nearly dying was punishment enough.

My mind wanders back to the man who saved me. I never learned his name, as he requested it be kept confidential. Apparently, he was wrongly imprisoned and later released, but not before he kept me from dying. I still wished I knew who he was—to thank him for more than preventing me from bleeding out that day. Because of him, I was released early and given a second chance at life. Albeit not the one I planned for myself, but a good one.

The vibration of my phone jolts me, and I glance down to see my sister's smiling face on the screen. She's the baby and by far the wildest of all four of us—even makes Dallas, our brother who runs a sex club, look like a girl scout, and that's hard to do.

"Hey, Twinkie. What's up?"

"How many times do I have to tell you not to call me that fucking nickname, Ryker? I'm not four anymore."

"You'll always be Twinkie to me, baby sis. Now, what's got you callin' me at,"—I glanced at my watch—"at three in the afternoon? Shouldn't you be at work or something?"

Mumbling what I'm sure is profanity under her breath, she grunts. "Well… I sorta got fired today… so, no. I'm not at work."

"Fired?" I sit up straighter. "Why'd you get fired?"

"One of the customers thought my ass was up for grabs, and I kindly showed him what happens when men make that assumption."

"Jesus. Do I need to call our attorney?"

"Nah. They let me go and gave him free food. I hated that job, anyway. But that's not why I'm calling you. Someone with an attorney's office left me a message. Said she needed to speak with one of us about family business. You know anything about it?"

"She leave a number?"

"Yeah." Danika rattles off the digits as I scribble them down on a pad. "I can call her back."

"Nope. I'll do it. It's probably another firm hoping to hit payday with a lawsuit against the state. It doesn't matter how many times I tell them no, they keep calling. I guess they've resorted to calling you guys. I'll see if Griffyn or Dallas have heard from anyone. This shit needs to stop. I have no interest in dealing with that type of bullshit. I just want to put it behind me."

"I hear ya, big brother. Alrighty… I need to head out and find a new job. Call you later, Ry-Ry."

Chuckling, I shake my head. "Love you, Twinkie. Stay out of trouble."

"Love you."

Disconnecting the call, I scrub my hand down my face and lean back in my chair. This shit with the blood-hound attorneys is getting out of control. I didn't want to sue the state then… and I sure as hell don't want to do it now.

I'd be a happy man if I never have to deal with another attorney for the foreseeable future. I want to get on with my life with no drama. The next time one of these motherfuckers calls me, I'll set them straight. In no uncertain terms will I be suing anyone anytime soon.

2

Addison

SLAMMING THE PHONE DOWN, I let out a frustrated scream. The sound echoes off my tiny office walls as I close my eyes and sigh in defeat. This is proving to be much more complicated than I thought. I don't know why I thought I, a junior attorney, could get anyone in this family to return our calls. Hell… the senior partners haven't been able to get them to respond. I don't know why I thought I could.

Oh… I know. I thought this would be my ticket out of being *a junior* attorney at this firm. When I overheard them talking about how desperate they were to get ahold of the Nash family, I thought it was my chance. How fucking wrong I was. The Nashes hate attorneys. Most likely stemming from the ambulance chasers who've hounded the youngest son, trying to convince him to sue the state of Alabama. Any lawyer worth his or her salt would know a suit against a state agency was a lost cause and a massive waste of time.

But this isn't that. This is something way more life changing, and I want to be the one to notify them. Sure, it's for selfish reasons, but in the end, this news could change everything for a family with a harder-than-necessary life. Sure, they're all doing well for themselves, but this news could be the start of something better for them.

Tapping my pencil on my desk, I stare at the Nash family file. They refuse to call us back or take our calls. There has to be another way to get them to listen to me.

"I see your brain burning over there." Libby, my best friend and fellow junior attorney, leans against the door frame, smiling. "I take it your big plan isn't working out as you hoped?"

"Ugh, no. No one is returning my messages, and the latest brother hung up on me before I could tell him why I was calling. Fuck those idiot dime-store lawyers for making him loathe any attorney who calls him. What am I going to do, Libby? I need this to show the partners I'm more than a lowly attorney. I'm tired of the bullshit cases they throw on my desk. If I can do this, they'll see I am ready for more."

"Maybe you're going about this all wrong. Maybe you need to think outside the box."

"What do you mean? Short of showing up at their place of work, I don't know what else to do."

Libby arches a brow, and I can see the wheels turning in her eyes.

"Why don't you?"

"Why don't I *what*?" I narrow my gaze at her.

"Show up at their job?" She moves into my office and plops down on the chair. "The partners certainly won't stoop that low. Them go out and find someone? Not going to happen, even if this is a big deal."

"Are you seriously telling me to travel a few hundred miles to Nashville and surprise one of the Nash brothers in person?"

She shrugs. "I'm sure Mr. Abernathy would approve the travel expenses when you tell him what you're doing."

"I can't tell them. They have no idea I'm even looking into this case file."

Shaking her head, she laughs. "They know, Addi. Those old farts don't miss much in this office. They probably haven't said anything, hoping you'd luck out and get one of them to come here. Then they'd take the credit for it. I don't know why you're so hellbent on being a partner here. This place sucks."

"Wow, Libby. I had no idea you felt that way."

"I need a job, so I keep it to myself." She pushes to her feet. "But as soon as I get the chance, I'm jumping ship. This place is stifling. What's it going to be, Addi?" She pauses at the door. "You gonna sit there and let the old balls dictate your worth, or are you going to do something bold and get what you want... even if it's here in this tomb of an office?"

I watch as she walks out, leaving me to ponder her suggestion. She's probably right, which is why I find myself heading toward Mr. Abernathy's office with the Nash file in hand. The worst they can say is no... actually, they could fire me for touching a case that wasn't mine. I'm banking on the fact they want this case closed, and they're tired of dealing with it.

Pausing outside his door, I tap my knuckles across the wooden barrier. The faint sound of Mr. Abernathy calling me inside filters through, and I push open the door.

"Miss Quincy." He swivels his chair to face me. "Come in and sit down."

"Sorry to bother you, Mr. Abernathy, but I wanted to run something by you."

"This about the Nash file you've been working on?"

His smirk makes my inside coil with nerves.

"Um... yes. I know I'm not assigned to it, but I thought I could try to help you by contacting them."

"And have you... gotten in contact?"

"Ah... no. It would appear the Nashes have developed a dislike for attorneys since Ryker Nash's incarceration."

"Yes,"—he nods his head knowingly—"we've encountered that same roadblock."

"Well..." I take a deep breath. "That's why I'm here. I have an unorthodox idea that may work."

"Okay." He leans back in his chair and fiddles with a pen, his gaze assessing me. "Let's hear it."

"What if I go to Nashville and try to speak with them in person? Maybe it'll force them to finally talk to us about this case, and we can finally bring it to a close."

"You understand that this case is sensitive, right? Showing up in person with this information may lead to some serious anger. Are you sure you're ready for that? Hanging up on us or returning mail is one thing. Cussing you to your face is another. Besides, it's not like we're losing anything by letting the file sit."

I understand what he's saying. It bothers me they don't seem to recognize the urgency of what's in the file.

"While that may be true, don't you think they deserve to know? I mean, this isn't just about an inheritance. It's about—"

He raises his hand to stop my words. "I know damn well what it's about. But I'm not spending time or money to hunt them down. Eventually, one of them has to answer a call or open a damn letter."

"Or I could go see them."

He holds my gaze for a moment. "Why do you want to do this?"

"I'm worth more than the patsy cases you've been giving me. I want to make partner at this firm, and chasing injury cases won't show you I am deserving."

"I see. And if it backfires and we've wasted money allowing you to chase something that can wait?"

"I won't fail," I say, shrugging my shoulders.

"Confidence can be a death sentence, Miss Quincy."

I sit, watching him watch me. His piercing gaze makes me squirm in my seat, and I start to wonder if I made a mistake coming in here like this. I'm just a lowly junior attorney. I've practically demanded they let me do this. Thinking I've made a mistake, I start to speak.

"Look, forget I came in here. It was a stupid idea, and I shouldn't have wasted your time."

"You're giving up already? Funny." He leans forward and narrows his gaze at me. "I was starting to think we might've overlooked someone promising for partner after all."

"No. I'm not giving up. I'll just do it on my own. I have vacation time."

He laughs, the sound making me cringe.

"No need, Miss Quincy. I'll grant you your request. But know this.... fail at this, and *partner* won't be the only thing you lose out on."

I blink in shock. "Wait… you're going to let me go to Nashville?"

"Yep." He grabs his phone. "But mark my words, Miss Quincy. When this little experiment fails, you'll wish you hadn't pushed this stupid idea. The Nash case is not worth the nightmare it's going to brew. I hope you're ready for it because when you uncap the lid to the reason we haven't been pursuing this matter, you'll wish you weren't born."

Gasping at his callous words, I push to my feet and stand. "You don't think they deserve to know about the will? About their inheritance?"

"Oh, you sweet, naïve girl. That is only the icing on a clusterfuck of a disaster." He reaches into his bottom drawer and thumbs through some files he stores there. "Here's the full fill. You have what we wanted in the open, but it's just the beginning to the end of many truths those boys believe. Now, you're going to be the one to destroy everything they thought they knew about themselves." Mr. Abernathy shakes his head. Stretching the folder across his desk, he holds it out of reach for a moment. "No backing out, Miss Quincy. Remember, sometimes, things are better left alone."

Gripping the file in my hand, I straighten my shoulders and hold his gaze.

"I won't back out."

Laughing again, he points me out the door. "Go… get your travel sorted out. In good faith, I'll even give you a month to get them here. Once you crack open that file, Miss Quincy, you'll need to rethink how you're going to deliver that blow. If I were you, I'd seek out the brother who will be the least trouble for you. Granted, I don't know which Nash that would be. Either way, good luck. Oh, and Miss Quincy?" I turn to look over my shoulder. "Shut my door on your way out."

Pulling the door closed, I cradle the heavy file against my chest and blow out a breath. I'm starting to wonder if I've bitten off more than I should with this case file. The folder I have access to only said they were due an inheritance they knew nothing about. Hearing Mr. Abernathy's warning has me worried I'm about to step into a hornet's nest of family drama.

Hurrying to my office, I toss the ticking time bomb down on my desk and pace. Libby peeks her head in and smiles.

"Well... what did stuffy dick say? He gonna let you go find the family?"

"Yeah, but now I wonder if it's a mistake. He talked about this case in such a way, I'm starting to worry it's more than about money due to them. He handed me that and said the entire file was under lock and key, so the contents wouldn't be leaked by anyone in the office."

Libby's eyes widen. "What the fuck? That's crazy. You sure saggy balls wasn't just trying to scare you?"

"Wow, you really hate him, don't you?"

"You have no idea, but that's not important. What is important is getting you packed and you reading that bible of a folder. Being prepared is the best way to approach them with whatever is inside. You need me to book you a hotel?"

"Actually, find me a rental. He's giving me a month to get this done."

"A month?" Her eyes widen more. "Holy fuck... what's in that folder, Addi?"

Closing my eyes, I sigh. "I have no idea... and that scares the fuck out of me."

"Why do I feel like he's sending you to the slaughterhouse?"

I couldn't agree with her more. Mr. Abernathy was all too keen on letting me make contact with the Nash family. Now, I wonder if Libby's analogy is spot on—only it sounds like I won't be the one left bleeding from the news held inside that manilla file folder.

The feeling I'm about to rip open a dark family secret weighs heavily on my heart… and I'm starting to wonder if this is the prelude to disaster. I can only hope I don't wind up destroying a family over my need to make partner with the firm. Breaking the Nashes might break me.

3

Ryker

Ducking Axel's uppercut, I dodge to the left and strike out with my right arm. The hit knocks him back, giving me ample time to adjust my stance. Stepping toward him, I finish the match with a quick one-two punch, leaving him laid out on the ground.

"Shit." I reach my arm down, holding my hand out to help him up. "You okay?"

Axel pops up with my help and shakes off the blow.

"It hurt, but I'll live. Besides, how am I supposed to get ready to win a belt if I can't handle your hits?" Axel smirks. "I gotta run, so same time tomorrow?"

"Yep." I slip between the ropes of the ring and jump to the floor. Grabbing a towel, I wipe the sweat coating my brow as I uncap my water and guzzle the liquid in one go.

As I go around the front desk, Christy is watching me. She's starting to get desperate and flirts a bit too much for my liking. If I was anything like my brother, Dallas, I would bend her over the desk and fuck her silly, but that was the old me. Since being in jail,

I've strayed from sex with women who only see me as the 'Saint.'" I don't want a relationship, and if I did, it wouldn't be with a woman like her. Mixing business and pleasure backfires, and I've had too many problems without workplace relationships being one of them.

The session with Axel went a bit longer, but it was good. The gym will be closing soon, and after my shower, I'll head over to the bar and seek a random hookup. If I can't find a quick fuck there, I'll go to my brother's house and hang out with him. Griffyn is the oldest and by far the most stubborn. As anti-relationship as I am, he multiplies that feeling by a quadrillion.

Stripping off my clothes, I flick on the showerhead and step beneath the water. The initial cold blast creates goosebumps on my skin, but they quickly dispel as the temperature heats to near scalding. I pump some of the body gel from the dispenser hanging on the wall and lather my hands. Coating my body in the suds, I let the spray wash over me, rinsing away the sweat and the strain of tonight's sparing match. Lost in thought, I don't hear the door to my office bathroom open.

"Thought maybe you needed some help in here." Christy's voice ricochets off the tiled walls. When I glance over my shoulder, she's standing completely nude behind me.

"What the fuck, Christy? You need to leave… now."

"Don't be like that." She takes two steps forward and presses her hand against my back. "I know you want me. I see how you glance at me. Let me make you feel good, Saint."

And there it is, the reason she's throwing herself at me. The title, not me, lured her into the shower.

"I don't know what you *think* you've seen, Christy, but I can promise you it's not desire."

Her hand moves down my stomach and grips my cock. "This says otherwise."

"I'm a man, Christy." Scoffing at her boldness, I grab her hand, halting her pursual of my dick. "When a naked woman stands in front of me, my dick is going to notice. It's biology, but it doesn't change the fact you've come into *my* private shower without being asked. I don't want you, now or ever." I slap her hand away as I move out from beneath the water and cut off the spigot. Pushing around her, I grab my towel and wrap it around my waist. Christy follows me out, not listening to my request for her to get out. "What part of 'get the hell out' did you misunderstand?"

Christy steps forward and jerks my towel off as she drops to her knees. She grips my cock before I can react and slides her mouth over the tip. My body responds almost instantly, but my brain catches up to what's happening, and I grab her hair.

"Stop, *Christy*."

The anger in my tone causes her to stop, giving me the opportunity to pull free of her grasp and mouth, the movement causing her to fall on her ass.

"You have about ten seconds to get your ass out of here."

"Seriously?" She glances up at me. "Why don't you want me?"

"My days of bedding women who only see me as Saint are over." I gather her discarded clothes strewn across the floor and toss them at her. Wrapping my towel around my waist, I jerk open my door and point to the hallway. "You can gather your shit when you go. You're fired, Christy. And if you think for a second about turning this into something more, remember, I have cameras everywhere. Including the showers."

Her face pales as she scrambles to stand, covering her bare breasts with her arms.

"Fuck you, Ryker. You're not all that, anyway."

I watch her bolt from the room and vaguely hear the front door shutting. Grabbing my clothes, I tug them on and close my eyes. Running my palm down my face, I blow out a frustrated breath. Maybe Luke was right—I need to get laid.

Once I secure the gym, I climb on my ride and head toward the local pub. Maybe picking up a piece of tail would ease this frustration that's riddling my body to the extreme. The night air cools my skin, burning off some of the pent-up anger I still have after Christy's bullshit encounter. I'd be lying if I said her lips didn't feel pretty good wrapped around my cock, but she's nothing but a nightmare wrapped in a pretty package.

The parking lot is packed, which means there's a good chance I'll be able to relieve the ache behind my zipper. The sound of music pours out of the door as I pull it open and step inside the bar. Navigating my way through the crowd of bodies, I saddle up to the bar on the last empty stool.

"Ryker." Jax, the bartender, sets a napkin down in front of me. "Haven't seen you in a while. How's it going?"

"Same ole, same ole. Business seems to be doing alright, I see." Glancing around, I scan the dance floor.

He chuffs out a laugh. "You haven't been in a while. Business is *always* like this on Fridays."

Nodding, I turn back to him and smile. "Can I get a Crown on ice?"

"You want a tab started?" Jax grabs a glass from beneath the counter and turns it up on the bar top. He scoops some cubes into it and then covers them in the smooth amber liquid.

"Nah, I'm not staying long." I toss him a twenty and smile. "Keep the change."

"Holler if you change your mind."

He scurries off to help some other patrons, leaving me alone in my thoughts. Just as I tip the glass to my lips, a hand presses into my back and drifts up and over my shoulder. Glancing back, my eyes lock with a pair of heavily lined eyes.

"Hey, sexy." The woman slips between me and the person sitting next to me. "You looked lonely over here."

Her tawny hair hangs over her bare shoulder, the tips resting against her chest. The dress she's wearing does very little to cover her body, but I'm sure it's intentional. For a minute, I consider brushing her off, but my dick seems to have perked up at the sight of her massive tits.

"Just watching the bar for something interesting." I practically eye fuck her. "Are you *interesting?*"

She giggles, a sound that nearly undoes the pulsating need in my pants, but I ignore it.

"I can be whatever you want."

Downing the last sip of my whiskey, I grab her hand and drag her across the dance floor and down the hallway. I've done this before, so finding my destination is like muscle memory. Shoving open the back door, we nearly tumble out into the alley, our anticipation of what's coming driving us forward.

"Seriously? The alley?" She cocks her head and blinks.

"You want my cock or not?" I'm not in the mood to deal with a whiney girl. Pushing her against the brick wall, I shove my knee between her legs and shove her dress up, pinching her nipples when they spring free. "If you want to stop, say so now because I plan to fuck you hard in about ten seconds." I reach into my back pocket and fish a condom out of my wallet. Unsnapping my pants, I shove them down slightly and sheath my already hard dick in the rubber.

"Turn around." I spin her around so she's facing away from me. "Brace your hands on the wall, doll. This is going to get rough."

"What—"

I rip her panties off and ram my cock between her folds, cutting her words off.

There's nothing gentle about the way I take her, but I don't care. She's a means to an end for me. Her whimpers echo off the alleyway as my shaft slams into her from behind. Her tits bounce beneath her shoulders as her head knocks into the bricks with each powerful thrust of my hips.

"Ow." She mutters, arching her ass toward me as she pushes away from the hard surface, impaling herself on my cock. "Oh my God." Her voice wobbles as her pussy clenches around my steel rod.

The sensation of her walls gripping my shaft spurs me on, and I don't ease up. In fact, my thrusts are unforgiving as I ram myself into her. My balls tingle as the sensation of my impending orgasm starts to move up from the base of my spine. Roaring out my release, I pull out of her and brace my hands against the wall.

"Fuck." I take several deep breaths to calm my racing heart as I stand at my full height. Gripping my softening dick, I pull off the condom and tie it off before tossing it into the nearby dumpster. Tugging my pants up, I move to step around the girl.

"Thanks, doll. I needed that."

"Wait." She nearly topples over as she hurries toward me when I head toward the main street. "That's it? You're just gonna fuck me and go?"

Pausing, I glance over my shoulder. "Did you think I was gonna date you? You weren't that great, sweetheart, but you did the job."

"Fuck you, Saint."

There it is. The only reason she wanted to fuck me. No one sees Ryker Nash… only the Saint. Shaking my head, I blow out a breath.

"Well, I guess you got what you wanted too, didn't you? Now you can run along and tell all your friends how Saint fucked you in the alley like a whore."

I hear her let out a string of expletives as I amble around the building and onto the sidewalk. She was supposed to take my mind off my shit day—instead, she's only added to it. Finding my motorcycle, I unfasten the helmet from the handlebars and slip it on my head. Straddling the seat, I fire up the engine and let the rumble of the engine work its way through my body. It seems my bed might be the only place I'll find peace for a little while.

Tomorrow is going to be a nightmare without a receptionist, but firing Christy was probably the only smart thing I've done tonight. Casting a glance toward the alley as I pull out, I'm relieved to see the girl, whose name I didn't even get, is no longer there. I might be a dick, but I wouldn't want her to get hurt by someone wanting to do nefarious things in an alleyway.

I snort at my thoughts. *Hell, I just did wicked things to her myself.*

Shrugging off the crappy night, I let the wind blow away my anxiety and head home. Since getting out of prison, I've felt restless, as if something is missing in my life. What, I have no idea. Maybe my brush with death changed my outlook on life. I know it's the reason I'm unwilling to step in the ring professionally again—being the *Saint* nearly cost me everything. Focusing on the lights of the city, I push down my depression. Maybe tomorrow, things will turn around.

They can't get any worse... can they?

4

Addison

I'VE BEEN in this town for twenty-four hours, and I'm hiding out in my hotel. Yesterday, I stopped by the college to try to speak with the eldest Nash, Griffyn, but his teaching assistant informed me he was in a meeting. Giving up, I came to the hotel, and last night, I hadn't fully accepted what I was doing.

Now, minutes from walking out of the safety of my room, the reality of what lies ahead is daunting. Until this morning, I hadn't bothered to Google all the Nash brothers. Yeah, stupid, I know. I assumed I'd be able to access Griffyn Nash with ease, seeing as he's a college professor, but that didn't pan out. I thought the information in the file was enough. Even if the photos were outdated significantly, I never imagined they'd look so different in person. Using the internet to track the rest of them down isn't—or wasn't—a priority until about twenty minutes ago. Being the intelligent woman I am, I figured knowing what Ryker Nash looked like now would be beneficial.

Now, I'm realizing the error in my previous judgment.

Ryker Nash, aka, The Saint, a boxing legend, is perfection. Standing at six foot two, the man is every girl's fantasy—hell, probably even some men. Being a professional boxer, his body is cut with ripples of muscles that seem never to end. His shaggy brown hair is cropped around the sides in a close buzz, leaving the top longer. His strong jaw lends to kissable lips that most women dream about. But that's not what has my heart beating like a racehorse—no, that would be the electric blue eyes that fall somewhere between cobalt and the color of the Caribbean ocean swirled together. Eyes even the camera seemed to focus on.

The mesmerizing orbs seem to lock a person into some kind of trance with very little effort. According to the article I found, Ryker Nash gave up professional boxing after the incident that resulted in his arrest. The recent photo I came across that was taken shortly after his release from being incarcerated shows a man who's haunted by demons. And here I am bringing even more to his doorstep.

Pushing down the fear and my body's sudden spark of desire, I slip on my red heels and straighten my black pencil skirt. Ensuring the white sleeveless silk blouse I don is tucked in, I grab my oversized handbag and shove the folder inside. As soon as I step inside the elevator, my nerves kick into overdrive. I can't fuck this up. My career and dreams are riding on successfully getting the Nash family to Atlanta to discuss the will they know nothing about.

Navigating through the parking garage, I grin at the sight of my ride —a Ford truck, sitting crooked in the space. Most people are shocked when they see me pull up in this beast of a ride, but I wanted something that made a statement, and this most certainly does for a woman who's barely five foot four. Yanking open the door, I toss my bag into the passenger seat and with very unladylike manners, hoist myself into the driver's seat. Keying in the address of his gym, I silently pray for this meeting to go off without a hitch.

Pulling into Strykers, I notice the parking lot is jam-packed with cars. He's obviously doing well, despite no longer being a professional boxer. Doing a shoddy job of parking, I give up and throw it in park. I grumble about the idiot taking up more than one space, making it nearly impossible to park my baby straight. After I slip my gallon tote over my shoulder, I slide out of the lifted truck and slam the door closed.

The building is definitely not what I expected. A modern red brick building, it's a lot larger than the gyms I've been to. *As if I go to the gym.* I mentally chastise myself for failing to work out like most women my age do. You'd think after the numerous times I've heard from the men I've dated how I'd be so much better if I would just lose a little weight, I'd maybe give the gym a try. But I haven't and don't plan on starting now. It's not like I'm a hippo, for Christ's sake. I'm on the shorter side with a good number of curves, even though those curves skipped my chest. Brushing my hand down my shirt, I take a deep breath and stride across the parking lot.

Jerking open the door, I'm assaulted by the sound of music mixed with the unmistakable sound of flesh hitting flesh. Stunned at the sight of two men pounding each other in the ring strategically placed in the center of the open floor plan, I stop in my tracks.

When my senses finally come back to me, I step over the threshold and amble toward the front desk. The counter is unmanned, making me furrow my brows. You'd think a place like this would have someone at the front at all times. Dropping my bag onto the counter, I turn around and lean against the edge. I can't seem to take my eyes off the man doling out punches like it's second nature to him. His head is covered in a protective helmet, making it hard to see what he looks like. It doesn't matter. My eyes are glued to him, regardless.

When his opponent gets knocked down, I watch in fascination as he bends over and helps him off the mat. My trance is shattered by the shrill sound of the phone ringing. No one seems to be in a hurry to answer the obnoxious interruption, but the sound is making me nutty. Scanning the space again, I shrug my shoulders, reach over the counter, and snatch the damn thing off its cradle, tired of hearing its annoying tone.

"Um… Hello?" Shaking my head, I clear my throat. "I mean. Strykers, can I help you?"

The person on the other end jabbers about needing lessons for his son, but I'm utterly clueless about how to answer.

"Sir, if you don't mind, I'm going to take your name and number and have the owner call you right back." Scribbling his info down, I set the receiver down and lay the paper beside it. As I turn to glance back at the boxing ring, my nose bumps into a wall of sheer muscle covered in a gleam of sweat.

"What the fuck are you doing?" The growly rumble of said chest causes my lady bits to tingle ever so slightly.

Squeezing my legs together, I stutter my response, "The phone was ringing… I…" My eyes slowly roam up the prodigious sight, lifting until I set my gaze on the most beautiful man I've ever seen.

"You what?" He folds his arms across the expansive mounds of perfectly sculpted skin and arches a brow over equally glistening sapphires.

"I was trying to help. You seemed tied up,"—I wave my hand toward the ring — "with all that."

"Well, you don't need to worry about interviewing. The job is yours."

I flinch at his statement. "I'm sorry... what?"

"I assume you're here because of the ad for a receptionist." His eyes peruse my body, making me stiffen. "Though you don't need to dress so uptight to work here. Jeans, shorts, hell, anything as long as you're not naked is fine. Let's go back to my office and talk about pay and all that."

Too dumbfounded to move, I watch as he heads in the direction of a set of stairs.

"You coming or not?" he asks, glancing over his shoulder. "I ain't got all day, doll."

Snapping out of the confusion, I grab my purse off the counter and fast walk to catch up to him.

"Wait. I think there's been some kind of misunderstanding."

My heels click against the metal stairs as I begrudgingly follow him up to his office. He flops down into his desk chair and stares at me expectantly.

"Miss..." he hesitates, waiting for me to fill in the blank.

"Quincy." I close my eyes and take a deep breath. "My name is Addison Quincy, but I—"

We're interrupted when a man steps into the office behind me.

"Shit, sorry, Ryker. But there's another law office on the line for you."

"Nope." He shakes his head. "Tell them I'm not interested. I'm fucking tired of these ambulance chasers trying to make a buck off me. I swear to God, I'm at the point of filing harassment charges on some of them. It's a damn good thing none of them have shown up here. I'd lose my shit and potentially visit lock up again. I just want to live my life in fucking peace." He glances at me and forces a smile. "Sorry for my language, Miss Quincy, but I'm sick and tired of attorneys hounding me."

"I see." I swallow down the bile in my throat.

"All right, boss. I'll run them off."

"Boss, huh?" Even though I already knew it was Ryker Nash sitting in front of me, I played dumb. "Nice gym you have here."

"Gym?" He chuckles. "It's a bit more than a gym, Miss Quincy."

"Please, call me Addison. Miss Quincy makes me think of my mother." I move to the chair opposite him and plop down. "Now... about downstairs—" I start, but he cuts me off.

"Look, I need a receptionist... badly. The last one attempted to slip her way into my bed... or shower, rather, and I fired her. I don't have time for women who want to bag the 'Saint.' I need loyal employees."

"The Saint?" I scrunch my face in confusion. "I don't follow."

Ryker stares at me with a look of disbelief. "You expect me to believe you don't know the 'Saint'?"

I lean forward. "Unless you're referring to the Archangel Michael... then no. I don't know who or what the 'Saint' is."

He leans back and watches me silently for a moment.

"Why would you come here for a job?"

I start to tell him that's not why I'm here, but his words echo in the back of my mind. *It's a damn good thing none of them have shown up here.*

I'd lose my shit and potentially visit lock up again. Which is the only reason I can come up with for what I'm about to say.

"I'm looking for a fresh start in life. Your position happened to pop up at the perfect time. I have experience dealing with clients." Of course, I don't tell him it's because I'm a lawyer. "And I deal with high levels of stress well. I'll be honest, it might be a temporary thing for me until I get some things settled."

"I don't care at this point." Smiling, he presses his elbows to the desk. "If you decide this isn't for you, I'll figure it out." He pulls out some papers. "Here's the pay. I need you to fill out these employment forms. When can you start?"

"Tomorrow." Snatching the stack of documents off his desk, I stand and grab my purse from the floor. "I'll bring these in tomorrow. What time should I arrive?"

Ryker stands and follows me. My body burns with awareness as he leans into me to pull open the door for me.

"Nine a.m."

I suck in a deep breath when his body brushes against mine.

"I'll be here." Looping my bag over my shoulder, I step out and start down the steps. He doesn't speak, but I can hear his footsteps behind me. Pushing the door open, I step into the sunlight and walk toward my truck. Ryker startles me by pulling open my door when I unlock it.

"Here, let me help you."

I hold my breath when he grips my sides and lifts me into the cab.

"Um… thanks." I smile awkwardly at him and toss my bag beside me. "I'll see you tomorrow, Ryker."

He steps back and closes the door. After cranking the engine and slowly backing out, I'm surprised to see him still standing there. His arms are hanging loosely at his side, but his gaze is locked onto the truck as I ease it out into the roadway.

As soon as he's out of sight, I blow out the breath I'm holding. Somehow, I've become his employee. This situation just went from difficult to dangerous in under an hour. I have to convince this man I'm there for a job when, in fact, it's all an act. I actually represent the exact thing he despises right now—a lawyer. That should terrify me, but it doesn't. No, what has me riddled with anxiety is that I'll be up close and personal with him, all while trying to earn his trust based on a lie.

What the fuck have I just done?

5

***

Ryker

After hiring Addison, I spent the rest of the day in my office. My thoughts were a jumbled mess about my new hire, and I couldn't quite figure out why, which is what led me to work this morning at the ass crack of dawn. At exactly eight forty-five, Addison Quincy walks through the front door, wearing a black sleeveless dress that hugs every curve she has.

Her dark locks are pulled into a tight ponytail once again, showcasing her gorgeous face. My eyes drop to the red stilettos showcasing her fantastic legs. It's all I can do to bite back a groan. Addison's five foot nothing frame is all curves. Her breasts are probably a handful at best, but her ass—fuck, I want to take a bite of that juicy rump. She's not the typical woman I go for, which strikes me as odd seeing as my dick seems to like her just fine. Adjusting the growing problem behind my zipper, I meet her at the counter.

"Morning, Addison." I give her a once over again and smirk. "A little dressed up, aren't you?"

She presses her hand against her hip and cocks her head. "Is there a dress code here? It wouldn't matter if I was working as a greeter at Walmart, Mr. Nash. I'd still want to look like a million dollars."

"Whatever." Throwing my hands up in surrender, I step back. "As long as you can answer the phones and handle scheduling for clients, I wouldn't care if you were in a trash bag. Now... let's get you set up." I wave toward the desk, stepping back to let her walk around me. As soon as she passes by, I regret my decision immediately. Her ass is perfection, and I want to sink my teeth into it.

Fuck, this girl is going to be a problem.

"So..." I slip beside her and point at the chair. "You'll sit here, answer the phones, and handle the scheduling system." I grab the mouse and wake up the computer. "This is where you'll put in client sessions and add new members. Once you do that, you set up billing, and it becomes automated."

She leans forward, her sweet scent filling my nose. Closing my eyes, I will my dick to behave. The last thing I need is another Christy issue, but damn if this woman doesn't have me in knots, and she hasn't even come on to me.

"Any questions?"

She shifts, causing her body to press into mine. Realizing her closeness, she steps back.

"Um, no, it's a lot like the one I use at work... I mean, my previous job." She smiles nervously at me. "You don't have to stay. If I get stuck, I'll just holler."

Backing up reluctantly, I tip my head and start toward the ring. "Thanks, Addison."

"My friends, call me Addi."

Her smile is like looking directly into the sun, and I can't help but stare at her. Without responding, I turn from the counter and nearly run smack dab into Luke.

"Who's the skirt?" Luke's eyes drift toward Addi.

Glancing over at her briefly, I shrug. "The new receptionist."

"New receptionist?" He snorts. "That girl looks uptight as fuck. You sure hiring someone that looks like her is a wise idea?"

"Right now, we need someone to man the desk. Yesterday, she answered the phone and handled it without having a clue as to what we do here. I hired her on the spot."

"I see..." Luke sucked his teeth. "Without even checking her background?" He shakes his head in disapproval. "I hope this doesn't turn into another disaster. A skirt like that isn't the type of woman you see in a boxing gym, Ryker. And a man like you should be cautious about who he lets into his life."

"I don't care what she wears as long as she doesn't try to suck my dick in the showers." Even as the words come out, there's a small part of me that wonders what her pouty lips would feel like wrapped around my cock. Giving myself a mental slap, I look at Luke.

"Right..." Luke chuckles as he slaps me on the back. "Then why are you just standing here, staring at her like you want to eat her?"

Shaking my head, I turn and head toward the ring dismissing his question entirely. "Come on. We've got shit to do."

Luke mumbles something as he follows behind me. Grabbing the ropes, I hoist myself onto the padded surface. Grabbing the gear off the stool in the corner, I strip my shirt over my head and slip the protective head and mouthpiece on.

"I need to spar. You in?"

"Hell, no." He holds his hands up. "I can see the tension in you, brother. Whoever is dumb enough to climb inside the ring right now deserves the beat down you're going to hand out."

"I'll do it," Axel smirks at me from the front door. He saunters over to the ring and tosses his bag on the ground. "If I'm going to be in the match at the end of the month, I need all the practice I can get."

"Whoa there." Luke grabs his arm, halting him in place. "Ryker's been going easy on you, Axel. Climb in there now, and I have a feeling you're going to get the Saint. You sure that's a good idea?"

"I've never been one for making good decisions." Axel glances between us and shrugs. "No reason to start now." He grabs the ropes and hurls himself beneath them. Pushing to his feet, he moves to the corner and tugs on some gear. "Just don't break anything."

Rolling my shoulders, I bounce from foot to foot as I warm up my muscles, Axel doing the same opposite of me. The moment I step into the center, Axel matches my movement. We dance around each other for a few seconds, but Axel shocks me with a quick jab to my center. Bouncing back, I throw my arms up in defense and taunt him with words.

"Lucky shot," I murmur. "Gonna have to do better than that to take me out."

The feeling of being back in the ring is overwhelming. I swore that after what happened, I wouldn't fight again, but the frustration coursing through my body needs an outlet, and this is the only way I know how to expel it.

It takes a few moments to find our rhythms, but before long, we're both pouring sweat as we move around the padded floor. Throwing uppercuts and jabs at one another, we're both panting from exhaustion. Axel looks weary on his feet, his eyes blinking to stay open. He takes a final swing at me, but it misses as I dodge it easily. I watch as he stumbles into the ropes.

"Let's call it." I throw my hands down, slinging off my gloves. Nodding toward the side. "Grab a shower, Axel. You did well."

Pulling his gloves off, Axel reaches for his helmet and grins. "That was fucking amazing. I can't believe I stayed on my feet with you, Ryker."

"He didn't give it his all," Luke quips. "Otherwise, you would be eating the mat right now."

Axel furrows his brows. "That true?"

"Probably." Shrugging his question off, I climb beneath the rails. "But it's not because I don't think you can handle it. I'm worried I can't."

As I climb out of the ring, I notice Addison watching me. Her gaze is completely focused on me, and for a moment, I stand there like a deer caught in the headlights of an eighteen-wheeler about to mow me down. I know I should move away, but I stand there, waiting for what I don't know. The clearing of a throat behind me snaps my gaze from her, and I turn to find Luke smirking. He flicks his eyes between Addison and me, his eyebrow raised in question.

Narrowing my gaze, I hurry around him into the back hallway and quickly dip into my office. Without stopping, I slip into my private bathroom and shut the door. I don't know what the fuck is happening to me, but I desperately want to shake off the weird-ass feeling snaking its way up my spine. Grabbing a towel from the closet, I sling it over the glass doors and turn on the water. As the steam fills the space, I smirk, knowing this time, I don't have to worry about Christy breaking in and trying to suck my cock.

Of course, thinking about my dick in someone's mouth conjures up the image of Addi.

God, she's *fucking* beautiful.

She's not the typical woman I go for—at all. Blonde hair, big boobs, and long legs are what I look for when desperate for a quick fuck. Addison Quincy is the complete opposite of that in every sense. At barely five foot five, her long caramel hair encases her face, highlighting her perfectly pouty lips. I swear to God, her curves remind me of a country road—one I would be happy to get lost on. The real kicker is she's got the juiciest ass I've ever seen. That delectable rump makes up for the fact she's lacking the normal double Ds I prefer. And that shit is messing with my head. I *never* go after a woman who isn't well endowed up top, but despite her short stature, all I can think about is her wrapping her perfectly shaped legs around my waist while I drill into her.

Easing into the massive walk-in stall, I stand beneath the spray and rinse off the sweat. My cock hardens more just thinking about Addison. Lathering my hand in the shower gel, I wrap my fist around my shaft and give it a tug. Thoughts of the siren manning the front desk cause my balls to tighten, and it doesn't take me long before I'm slamming my free hand against the wall and spraying my release across the tiles. As my body shudders through the orgasm, I cry out her name.

I'm so fucked when it comes to this girl.

Rinsing the cum from my hand, I wipe down the splatter of my release and turn off the water. I grab my towel and dry off. Wrapping the towel around my hips, I jerk open the door and step out.

A gasp paired with a muttered *'shit'* has me looking up. The star of my jerk-off session is standing at the open door. Her slack jaw hangs open as her eyes drop to my bare chest. I watch as she licks her lips, her gaze slowly lowering to my towel-covered dick—a dick that's now standing at attention. There's absolutely nothing I can do to hide the boner I'm sporting beneath the white towel wrapped around my waist.

"Um." Her eyes are transfixed on my cock, who has noticed she's in the room.

Regardless of just spending my load thinking about her in the shower, he's standing at attention like a recruit in basic training waiting for his orders to perform.

"The door was open, I-I..."

Her inability to form a sentence makes my dick jump with need. I'm about ten seconds away from cumming into this towel like a prepubescent boy seeing tits for the first time.

"My eyes are up here, sweetheart."

Hearing my voice, Addison's sultry gaze snaps to my face, giving me a bird's eye view into her emerald jewels, glittering with what I can only assume is desire. It's like a raging fire is burning in the depths of her orbs, as her cheeks are tinged red, knowing I am reading her like an open book.

"Sorry."

She blinks, trying to hide the primal reaction to seeing me almost nude, but it's too late because I see how she looks at me. I'm not stupid. I know how I look. I've worked hard for my body—one that has no trouble attracting women when I want one. Her gaze scans the black ink covering my chest, and I smirk as she licks her lips and lets her eyes drop once more to my waist.

"I'll come back." Spinning on her heel, she turns to leave, but there's no way I'm letting that happen.

"No." She freezes at my command. "Shut the door, Addison."

"Sir?" Her voice comes out in barely a whisper, and she keeps her back to me.

"Shut. The. Door."

I know I'm playing with fire, but I don't move as I wait for her to do as I ask. There's a strange electricity coursing between us, charging the room with a power I'm almost afraid to tap into. The thrum of what lies between us is making the hair on my arms stand on end. It's dangerous, but I can't stop myself from wanting more. It feels like forever, but Addi finally reaches out tentatively and pulls my office door closed. She doesn't face me, but I watch as her shoulders drop, and a sigh escapes her lips.

"I'm sorry. I didn't know you had a shower in here... nor did I realize you were in it. I needed to speak with you, and Luke directed me back here."

The motherfucker. He knew exactly what I was doing back here. There is no doubt he did this on purpose. And even though I want to be mad at him, I can't be—not when he's given me the opportunity to do *exactly* what I swore I wouldn't do.

"Turn around, Addison."

6

Addison

I SPENT most of the morning trying my best to ignore Ryker—keyword *trying*. It's like my eyes have a mind of their own and are constantly drawn to him. I watch as his friend Luke mumbles something to him, which in turn appears to irritate him. Ryker practically stomps across the floor and hurls himself into the ring.

Turning away when the phone rings, I focus my attention on the caller. After a few minutes, my cell phone vibrates in my pocket, and I tug it out to see Libby's face on the screen.

"Hey, girl." I sigh into the phone, turning my chair to stare out the glass windows at the front.

"How's *work*?" Her sarcastic tone filters through the line, making me chuckle.

Blowing out a breath, I push aside the disappointment in her voice and give the only answer I can. "Fine."

"I still can't believe you're doing this, Addi. What happens when he finds out why you're really there? It could blow up in your face."

My best friend is one hundred percent right. This shit only has one way to end, and it's not going to be pretty, yet here I sit, staring out the front window of Strykers.

"I know, but this just fell in my lap, and I couldn't see another way."

"You're a fucking junior partner, Addi. A lawyer. Not a receptionist."

"I get that, but he hates anyone associated with lawyers. He would have shut me down immediately, and coming here would have been for nothing."

My mind drifts to the file stuffed inside my purse. Everything about this damn case screams danger, but being here means I'll see this through to the end. *Too bad I don't have the foresight to know what the end will look like.* The Nash brothers deserve to know what's inside this damn will. Even if it's going to shake the very foundation they sit on. I close my eyes and try to focus on Libby's words, but it's nearly impossible.

The sound of someone clearing their throat jostles me out of my blank stupor. I glance up to see a large man standing in front of the counter. He's the very definition of a boxer, topping my small frame by at least seven inches. His shaggy black hair hangs over his dark eyes as he stares down at me.

"I gotta go, Libby." Shoving my phone into the desk drawer, I meet the customer's irritated gaze and smile. "Sorry about that. Can I help you?"

"Where's Christy?"

Furrowing my brows together, I vaguely remember her name being mentioned as the former receptionist. "She no longer works here."

"Oh." He glances to the side, contemplating his next words. "Well… she would… uh." He swallows nervously. "She would always sign me in." He leans onto the countertop and winks.

Tilting my head to the side, I let my eyes wander over his massive frame. He's an attractive man, with ripples of muscle, and based on the way he's leering at me, he's obviously used to getting what he wants from a woman. But I'm not like most women and could give two shits about his looks or giving him something because of them. In fact, I despise men who think they're God's gift to women.

"Well, just give me your name, and I'll take care of it."

He straightens, shifting on his feet. "My name? Why? She never needed it before. She'd just wave me through."

"I see." Shaking my head. "Well, I'm new, and I don't know you, so your *name,* please."

"Justin Branch." He sighs. "But you're not going to find a membership. Christy and I had an arrangement."

"An arrangement?" I cock an eyebrow at him.

"Look, princess." He leans forward again. "I'd fuck her, and she'd let me in for free. But since she's not here… I can certainly make the same arrangements with you."

Snorting, I roll my eyes at him and push to my feet. "Justin, was it?" I lean against the edge of the counter, getting closer to him, so he can hear me more clearly and plaster on my *'you're a dick,'* smile. "I am not interested in any *kind* of arrangement with you other than your monthly membership payment. But since you've obviously been coming to this establishment for God knows how long for free… I'm going to have to ask you to leave."

"You're kicking me out?"

"Yes." I sit back down and begin typing on the keyboard, searching for his information. "I've also *found* your inactive account and made a note that you're banned from the premise."

"You can't do that. I want to talk to Ryker."

Standing back up, I narrow my gaze at him as my arms fold across my chest.

"Need I remind you what you were doing was illegal? I'll happily get Mr. Nash for you, but know he's liable to call the cops." Turning my head, I scan the gym, my gaze landing on Ryker mid-swing.

My mind completely blanks out, and I vaguely hear the door chime as it slams shut and the jackass departs from the premises. Instead, I'm riveted to the panty-melting sight before me. Beads of sweat roll down the ridges of muscle flexing on Ryker's back as he moves around the mat. I watch as his ribs stretch and expand with each deep breath he takes. As my eyes take the journey up his delicious frame, they come to a stop at his piercing indigo gaze—a gaze that's laser focused on me. A tiny smirk appears at the corner of his lips. I swear bells are ringing as my lady bits clench between my legs. It's like we're trapped in some parallel universe, and no one else exists but me and him.

It isn't until his friend, Luke, steps beside him and slaps him on the shoulder that the trance between us is broken. Luke rolls his eyes at him as he whispers something into his ear, making Ryker's expression fill with irritation. The real-world washes over me like a tidal wave, and the sounds of the gym force my senses back just as he storms off toward his office.

"Ryker." I call out his name, realizing I needed to talk to him about the muscled jerk and former employee stealing from him. My plea for him to stop falls on deaf ears. "Shit."

"If you'd stared any longer, I'm pretty sure you'd have burst into flames." Luke ambles toward the counter, laughing. "I thought I was going to need to call the fire department on you two eye-fucking each other so hard."

"I've never seen anyone box before… I mean, other than on television." I shrug. "He makes me wish I'd taken up the sport as a serious spectator."

"Really?" Luke shakes his head. "Addison, I'm not sure what game you're playing, but don't fuck with him, okay? He's had enough bullshit to last a lifetime, and he doesn't need someone coming in here and messing with his head."

"What's that supposed to mean?" I move around the counter and press my hands into my hips as the toe of my heel taps against the concrete floor. "I needed a job, and he was kind enough to give me one."

"A job." Luke chuckles. "A girl that dresses like you doesn't belong in a gym. But he likes you… why I don't know, because a man like Ryker will eat you alive."

"It's not like that between us." I fold my arms across my chest and glare at him. "I'm not Christy. I have zero desire to get in your friend's pants."

"When Ryker wants something, he takes it." Luke shakes his head, disbelief covering his face. "And you, Addison, are something I think he wants—even if he hasn't admitted it to himself yet."

"Well… he's going to be disappointed. I'm not an object to be had. Now,"—I spin on my heel—"I need to speak with him."

Luke waves his hand toward the hallway. "Go on back to his office. I'll watch the desk for you."

Practically stomping away from him, I scurry down the hall to his office. "Ryker?" I call out as I tap on the partially open door. Pushing it open all the way, I step inside and nearly trip over my feet when I come face to face with the biggest temptation of my life.

Wrapped in nothing but a towel, Ryker steps out of what I assume is a bathroom. His body is glistening with water, and his hair is still wet. I inhale a breath, which comes out more like a gasp. I mutter something, but I'm too hyper-focused on the perfection that's his body. I know my fucking jaw is hanging wide open, but that doesn't stop my gaze from dropping to his perfect chest covered in black ink. Licking my lips without thinking, I let my eyes wander down to the tent below his belly button.

"Um." I'm unable to peel my eyes off his magnificent towel-covered dick. A dick that no man should be allowed to possess. "The door was open, I-I..."

"My eyes are up here, sweetheart."

The grumble of his voice makes me quiver, both from embarrassment and desire. My face feels hot, which means he knows exactly what I'm thinking. Peeling my gaze from the California Redwood threatening to tear the cotton material concealing it, I look at him sheepishly.

"Sorry."

But my words have no meaning as I take one more look at the package nestled between his legs. It is as if my eyes have their own damn mind, and all they can think about is his massive cock. Forcing myself to turn away and move to the door, I call out over my shoulder like a coward.

"I'll come back."

"No." I swear to God, he growls the command, making my entire body seize up. "Shut the door, Addison."

Closing my eyes, I try to replay what he said, but I'm completely focused on vacating his office before I do something stupid.

"Sir?"

"Shut. The. Door."

Here goes something stupid. There's some sort of sickness inside me, and I can't stop the desire to turn around and face him, knowing it's going to wreck me. Instead, I force myself to keep my back to him and push the door closed, bracing my palms against the wood for support.

"I'm sorry. I didn't know you had a shower in here… nor did I realize you were in it. I needed to speak with you, and Luke directed me back here."

"Turn around, Addison."

Car meet collision.

Taking a deep breath, I turn to the man of any girl's fantasy. Purposefully, I keep my gaze on his face and not straying to the muscle I want him to choke me with.

"I can come back."

Ryker takes two steps toward me and cages my body against the door. The closeness of his nearly naked flesh sends electric tingles across my skin, and I keep my eyes trained on the pools of blue threatening to consume me. Ryker is a walking firestorm of danger. This man shouldn't have this effect on me in such a short amount of time, but the moment I met him, I knew I'd willingly get burned for just one touch.

"Do you make it a habit of walking into someone's office when you didn't ask for permission?"

"Ask?" I blink, my brows knitting together in frustration as I look to the side. I did knock… kind of. "The door was open, Ryker. I had no idea you had a shower in here nor that you were using it."

"Look at me, Addison." I turn my confused glare back to his face. "Did you come in here hoping I would want to fuck you, or maybe I'd let you suck my cock?"

Gasping at his crude remark, I firmly press my hand into his chest and shove him back slightly.

"Fuck you, Ryker. Just because your previous employee was a slut, doesn't mean every other woman is one, too." Ducking under his arm, I walk toward his desk and turn, pointing my finger in his direction. "I came in here to tell you Christy was basically stealing from you—but obviously, you think I came in here to drop my panties or try to suck you off. Well, let me clear that up for you, boss. My panties are firmly in place." *Lie.* "And I wouldn't suck your dick now… or ever. God knows who all you've stuck it into."

Ryker stiffens, and I watch with a shocked and confused look as he turns the lock on his door. A moment of panic washes over me, and I start to back up, creating some distance from him as he stalks toward me with a primal look in his eyes.

"What are you doing?"

"Don't worry, *princess*. I don't force women to do anything they don't want to." He steps in front of me and presses his palm to my cheek. "But the way your eyes dilate and the rapid beating of your heart right here,"—he presses his thumb against my throat—"tells me you're a liar."

"You're wrong," I whisper, knowing damn well he's right. God, if he knew how wet my panties are right now, he'd be gloating like the arrogant prick he is.

"Am I?" He guides me backward until my knees hit the edge of the desk. Ryker slowly presses me against the wood, caging me in place. "Are you saying if I were to reach beneath that uptight skirt you have on, I wouldn't find you wet for me?"

Swallowing, I take a breath and pinch my eyes shut, trying to ignore the pulsing need between my thighs. "I-I…" Stuttering, I can't seem to find the words to tell him he's wrong, mainly because even as fucked up as this moment is… he's right.

"That's what I thought."

I whimper as he slides his hand up my leg and beneath my skirt. The pads of his fingertips feel rough against my flesh as he bunches the material up, exposing my satin panties. He pulls the fabric up, holding it in one hand as his free hand blazes an inferno across my hip.

"You want to know what fucking the *Saint* is like, don't you?"

"What?" I can't stop myself from leaning back as his thumb brushes across the swollen nub beneath the smooth material.

Ryker leans his head beside my ear and whispers. "I'm not that man anymore, Addison. I don't fuck girls who want a piece of the Saint."

The cold air brushes against me as he steps away from my body, leaving me smoldering from his touch. Peeling my eyelids back, I blink in shock. The lust that once filled my gaze is suddenly replaced with anger… no *rage*. Pushing off the desk, I jerk my skirt back in place, smoothing out the material as I right myself on my heels. Straightening my spine, I pierce the selfish prick with a look, so he knows exactly what I'm feeling.

"Fuck you, Ryker. I didn't come in here for you to humiliate me like this. As I said, I'm not a whore. I *was* trying to save your business, but you can figure that shit out yourself."

As I move to leave, Ryker darts beside me and presses his hand against the door, keeping me from opening it.

"Shit, Addison. I'm sorry. Please don't leave."

When I see he's not going to budge and let me leave, I take a step back and wrap my arms around my waist. I don't want him to see me as weak, but fighting back the tears threatening to fall is becoming difficult.

"I don't know what the hell that was about, Ryker, but I'm not some two-bit whore who took this job to land you in bed. And the 'Saint'? I didn't even know who that was until you offered me a fucking job." *Partially true, I mean, I did look him up before coming here.* "I had to go home and research you and this place. Coming in here was a fluke." *Another lie.* "You offering me a job on the spot was completely unexpected, but I won't work here if you're going to treat me like I'm trash."

"Fuck." He fists his hair, the towel precariously hanging off his hips. At that moment, I realize how dangerously close it is to falling off. Seeing my gaze fall to the towel, Ryker's hand goes to the material. "Can you give me a minute to throw on some clothes, then we can talk?"

"Whatever."

He darts into the bathroom again, this time carrying some clothes. As soon as the door shuts, I blow out a frustrated breath. I should walk out of here and just say fuck it, but I would be throwing away my dreams of becoming a partner if I did. I can't decide if I'm madder at what he did or at the fact I liked it.

Jesus Christ, I'm screwed either way.

The minute Ryker finds out who I am and why I'm really here, he's going to hate me even more than he already does.

7

Ryker

Fuck.

I jerk on my shorts and pull the t-shirt I'm fisting over my head. My rash decision led to me practically forcing myself on Addison. I was certain her presence was a repeat of Christy, but the expression on her face when I said I didn't fuck girls who only wanted the Saint nearly knocked me on my ass.

When she lit into my ass and started to storm out, I knew I'd been the one to fuck up. Now, staring at my reflection, I can't help but wonder who was staring back. Splashing some cold water on my face, I took a deep breath and opened the door.

Addison is perched on the edge of the couch in my office. Her body is stiff, similar to the way the nuns used to sit in the front row at mass when mom made us go. It shows she doesn't really want to be here. Guilt assuages me, and I falter in my steps at the notion I'm the reason she suddenly looks so unhappy. Hearing me exit the bathroom, Addison's head turns in my direction. Her expression is even worse than her posture. The redness of her eyes is a definite giveaway that she is fighting back tears.

"Shit, Addison." I move quickly to pull a chair in front of her. Straddling it backward, I rest my forearms on the back and sigh. "I owe you an apology. The way I acted was completely inappropriate, and I wish I could take it back."

"You're kidding, right?" she snaps as her head shakes. "I think me being here isn't going to work. I'm sorry, Ryker, but you were right. I don't belong." Her words come out rapid-fire.

"Whoa." I held up my hands for her to slow down. "Hang on there, Addison. I made a snap judgment a few minutes ago, and it has nothing to do with you and everything to do with me. While I'll admit you're not like the typical women who've worked here before, that doesn't mean you don't belong."

Addison bites down on her lip, thinking over my words. "I…" She pauses. "Look, I didn't come here for a job, Ryker."

I narrow my gaze. "What do you mean?" My phone rings, interrupting our conversation. "Give me a second." Pushing up from my seated position, I grab my cell from my desk and press it to my ear. "Griffyn, what's up?"

"An attorney stopped by my office yesterday."

I glance at Addison, who is twisting her hands in her lap. The sight of her delicate hands creates a distraction causing me to miss what my brother says. "What'd you say? Sorry—I'm in the middle of something."

Turning my back to Addison so I can focus, Griffyn repeats himself.

"Jesus, Ryker. I said… an attorney came by my office yesterday. My TA was handling the class while I was stuck in a damn meeting with the dean."

"What the fuck? Now they're bothering the family?"

"I don't know. Justin just said some woman came by asking for me. Said she was with an attorney's office out of Atlanta and needed to speak with me."

"Atlanta? Jesus Christ. Did he get her name?"

"He was in the middle of a lecture when she knocked on the door—so no, he didn't get a name. All he said was she was your typical uptight-looking attorney."

Sighing as I run my fingers through my hair, "Fuck, this is getting old. Okay, if she comes by again, get a name. I'll take care of it."

"It's fine, Ryker. I can manage some attorney dressed in a *skirt*. I just wanted you to know about it in case she comes by the gym. I don't need you losing your cool with her."

"Yeah... I hear you. Alright, Griffyn. Keep me posted, will ya?"

"Sure. Come by the house... we can chill out with a beer."

Rubbing the back of my neck, I turn to see Addison staring at me wide-eyed.

"Shit. Look, I'll call you later when I'm headed over." After saying goodbye, I shove the phone into my pants. "Sorry about that. I kinda forgot you were in here."

"Everything okay?" She presses her hand to her mouth and nibbles on her nails nervously.

"I think so," I answer, smiling at her. "It's just these bloodsucking attorneys can't take a hint and leave me alone."

"Why are they hounding you?" Addison fidgets in her seat. "You being sued or something?"

"The opposite, actually. A while back, I was incarcerated and during my stay, I was attacked. Turns out the guards were paid off to turn their head the other way."

"Jail?" Addison bolts to her feet, like she's been caught with a criminal.

Seeing her anxiety build, I step forward and squeeze her shoulders.

"Hey… I fucked up and hurt someone by accident. Unfortunately, I was still found guilty of manslaughter. After the incident, the judge released me to avoid negative press. Even though I deserved to spend the whole sentence in prison, I got out."

"Oh." She glances toward the door, plotting her escape. "I should go."

"Addison. I don't want you to quit. What happened a moment ago was just me being a complete asshole. I shouldn't have touched you without your verbal consent, and for that, I'm sorry. I'm not that guy, I swear."

Addison holds my gaze, and I watch as her tongue darts out and smooths across her bottom lip. It takes all my willpower to keep from snagging her around the waist and claiming her lips.

"It's fine, Ryker. Really. I could have pushed you away, but I got caught up in the moment, too. Let's just forget it happened. Besides, you've made it clear I'm not like the women you usually fuck." Addison blinks and moves toward the door. "Let's just keep this a working relationship, *boss.*"

I watch as she slips out the door, mentally kicking myself for every-thing that just transpired. Even thinking about how I had my hands on her, my cock swells and tightens my shorts. She's right, though. She's not like the women I usually fuck around with. So, why can't I seem to get her out of my head?

Luke peeps his head around the wall and smirks. "How's it going in here, boss man?"

"Fuck you, Luke. You sent her in here, knowing full well I was likely going to be in the shower. You put her and me in an awkward position."

"Please, you might try to act like you don't want her, but I watched you with her. That woman is going to have you twisted in knots before long."

"I don't have time nor need another Christy, Luke. Not with attorneys harassing me and my brothers. Right now, I need to figure out who the hell is looking for me."

"Whoa, what the hell are you talking about?" Luke saunters into the room and flops down into one of the vacant chairs. "Who's looking for you?"

"Griffyn called. Some stuffy woman showed up at the college looking for him. Lucky for us, his TA was manning the class and, in not so many words, told her to fuck off."

"He get a name?"

"No." I shake my head. "He was in the middle of a lecture, and she interrupted. All he wanted to do was get her the hell out of there. So now you see why I don't have time for games. Some pretentious bitch is hounding the family. I'm so sick of these attorneys. When will they take a fucking hint I don't want to sue the fucking state?"

Luke and I chat a bit longer about the way these ambulance-chasing firms have come out of the woodwork. They see big dollar signs when looking at my case, but all I see is even *more* bad publicity. Maybe someone else would see lining their pockets on the state's dime, but I don't give a shit about that. I'm sitting okay with the winnings I earned from my career before it blew up in my face. I might have made a stupid decision that ended my professional career, but I've been smart with my investments. The thought of suing anyone turns my stomach.

Walking out of the gym after we close up, my mind is still on my brother's call. I'd hoped this shit would die down when I ran off the first couple of attorneys who showed up within weeks of my release, but now, nearly a year later, they're still trying hard to make a buck off my near life-ending incident.

As I get near my bike, my attention is snagged by the sound of a car door slamming. Turning in the noise's direction, I spy Addison slowly backing her massive truck out of her parking spot. That's another thing I've fucked up. She could have called the cops on me for what I did. She might not have said no, but she sure as shit didn't say yes. I'm not the kind of man to force a woman to fuck me, but something about her has me making all kinds of mistakes. Shrugging off the disgust, I climb onto my motorcycle and slip on my helmet.

I'm not in the mood to be around many people, so I head in the direction of my brother's house. Griffyn lives close to campus in a two-story house build in 1892. It needed a lot of work, but he redid everything on the inside. While the inside is modern and sleek, the outside reflects a storybook Victorian-style house. It makes me laugh knowing my brother lives inside something that looks like it fell out of a fairytale. He is definitely not someone who believes in fairytales.

Pulling into the driveway, I park and kill the engine. It's after ten, but Griffyn doesn't go to sleep until well after midnight. I wish it was because he had a woman, but it's not. He's devoted himself to his job, leaving little room for a social life. As soon as I reach the door, Griffyn pulls it open.

"Surprised you actually showed up." Stepping back, he waves me inside.

I follow him into the modest living room and pause. "When did you paint?" I glance around the space noting the new color. "I didn't take you for an aqua man."

"Let's just say I let my TA pick up the paint, and this is what I got."

Snorting, I shake my head. "Isn't he a dude? I mean, I guess in this day and age, turquoise might be a man's favorite color."

"I have more than one TA, and no, the paint wasn't picked out by Justin." Griffyn doesn't elaborate, and I sense there might be more to his aggravation, so I let it go. "Any issues with any more attorneys?"

"Nope. What more did Justin tell you about the broad who came to the college?"

"Not much. He was in a rush to get her gone. Said she was an older woman with brownish colored hair. That's it."

"I'm over these fuckers. You'd think after two years they'd let it go."

We spend the next hour shooting the shit. Griffyn suggests getting Dallas and Danika over sometime this week, but the likelihood of getting all four of us together at one time is slim. I often wonder if our father had lived if our lives would be different. Not that I'm complaining.

After our dad was killed in a car accident, my mother met Byron. He helped her pick up the pieces of her broken heart. Shortly after they got married, he asked to adopt us—Griffyn had a hard time with it at first, being seventeen, but finally acquiesced. Turned out to be the best thing he could have done. Byron was a former

Marine, and by adopting us, could use his veteran status to pay for our colleges. Not to mention a year after they married, we welcomed Danika into the family. Mom was overjoyed to have a girl —even if Danika is a tomboy a heart.

Bidding farewell to Griffyn, I climb on top of my motorcycle and make the trek to my house. It's nothing like Griffyn's house, but our tastes aren't exactly similar. He likes that old home feel, while I wanted something more modern. When I found this place up for sale, I jumped on it right away. Once an old warehouse, I paid a local contractor to convert it into a house. Parking the bike, I hop off and walk over to the panel on the wall. Keying in the code, the garage door lifts. Quickly hopping back onto my ride, I ease into the space, parking next to my Escalade.

After closing the massive door, I step inside. The cool brick interior offsets the metal exterior with sleek lines and wood accents. The kitchen is off the garage entry, which opens to the massive two-story living room. The dark gray concrete floors provide a sexy feel to the masculine style of my home. A huge screen television takes up most of the solid wall. Several picture windows have been cut out from the metal frame, giving me a perfect view of the woods behind my house. I had the designer intentionally leave the front of the warehouse alone, giving the illusion it's not something lived in.

Tossing my keys onto the counter, I grab a bottle of water from the fridge. Glossy black cabinets, adorned with discreet handles, conceal top-of-the-line appliances that blend seamlessly with the overall aesthetic. Rounding the dark marble island, I climb the wood and metal staircase to the second floor. The atmosphere up here takes on a more intimate and personal tone. Three rooms occupy the second level. A small bedroom, guest bathroom, and the master. Not bothering to change my clothes, I sit my drink down and drop onto the bed. My mind is a mess of emotions I can't control. Between the irritation of my family being harassed by attorneys for a quick payday and the desire I feel whenever Addison is around, I'm probably going to go crazy. Even as sleep claims me, the beautiful woman fills my thoughts.

I have to get control of myself. I don't have time for distractions... not even if the distraction is in the shape of Addison Quincy.

8

Addison

Ten days.

That's how long I've been pretending to be something I'm not. And instead of making things easier, I'm pretty sure I've made them worse. Between the lude comments from some of the gym members and the suspicious vibe Luke throws off every time he's around me, I'm ready to confess everything.

The guilt nagging at my conscious is exactly why I'm sitting here at the bar on my night off. I spent an hour on the phone with Mr. Abernathy this morning. He wanted an update, one I don't have, which led to him reminding me what's riding on my ability to get the case closed. A case, might I add, I asked to handle. *How stupid of me.* When I took this on, I had no idea what it entailed, not really.

It was supposed to be a simple inheritance case. Snorting at my thoughts, I press my lips and sip the sweet concoction I've been sucking down for the last sixty minutes. Rolling the information I've read over and over, I can't for the life of me comprehend how a man who left them their money had hid the multitude of things that he did. Hell, I'm having a hard enough time playing the role I'm trying to convince Ryker I fit into.

"Think maybe you should slow down?" The bartender's voice washes over me, and I glance up to find him staring at me.

"Are you my keeper?" I ask, cocking an eyebrow at him. "I'm fine… and not driving. So, how about you give me another one, *please?*" Rolling his eyes he shakes his head. I can see the hesitation in his eyes, but when I shove the glass at him, he concedes and takes it. "Thanks."

The bar is hoping for a Friday night, and part of me is considering a random hookup—something I never do. I need a distraction… one that doesn't involve complications.

"You look like you could use some company." The deep timbre voice startles me from my perusal of the patrons, and I glance over my shoulder to find a decent-looking guy smiling at me. "Can I buy you another drink?" He nods his head in the direction of my almost-empty glass.

"Um… Sure." I swivel to face his body, watching as he waves over the bartender. I don't miss the flicker of concern in his eyes as he takes our order.

"You here alone?"

"Not anymore." His cocky response causes me to roll my eyes. Sensing my disdain for his attempt at being suave, he clears his throat. "My friends are over there." He points toward a table in the corner and my gaze falls on several men and women engrossed in conversation.

Taking the drink from the bartender, I press the glass to my lips and sip it.

"What's your name?" I set the cup down, my motions slightly skewed as the liquor is really starting to hit.

"Chad. Yours?"

I muffle my giggle at hearing his name. *Chad*. What the fuck? I'm starting to wonder if I'm destined to attract men who believe loafers are Friday night attire. Glancing down at his feet, I pinch my eyes closed when I see he is in fact wearing loafers and no socks. Do I continue this conversation with him? I mean, he's not ugly, but...

He says something and I glance up.

"I'm sorry. What'd you say?"

"I asked your name."

"Addison." I swallow my irritation and plaster a fake smile on my face. "Look, Chad." I give my head a little shake, trying to clear the drunkenness from my brain as I wobble in my red stilettos. "I think I'm going to call it a night."

He stands at the same time I do. "At least let me walk you out."

"Sure." Shrugging my shoulders I leave a wad of cash on the bar and slip off the stool. "Thanks."

Chad moves behind me, and I can't help the involuntary wince when he places his hand on my back, ushering me out the front door. Slipping my phone out of my purse, I request my Uber. Chad, seeing what I'm doing, steps closer to my body.

"How about you save some money and let me take you home?"

Leaning back, I look up at him. "Thanks, but I'll wait for my Uber."

"I think we'd have a good time together, Addison." Chad backs me up, crowding me against the brick wall. "Come on... live a little."

Just as I move to press my hands against his chest, his body is wrenched away from me. I blink through the blurry fog of my intoxication in time to see a massive form slamming him on the ground. To my shock, Ryker is straddling Chad on the sidewalk, his fists poised to do maximum damage.

"Leave her the fuck alone."

The primal growl that comes out of him does two things at once. First, it causes utter fear in Chad, who is practically begging for him to get off. And two, I'm pretty sure I've either just pissed myself or came from the vibration of his voice. Neither are good options. I rush forward as Ryker drops his fist against Chad's nose, the disgusting crunch of bone and cartilage echoing into the night sky.

"Ryker!" I scream, reaching out to grab his arm—which I realize too late is a dumb idea.

Ryker's arm moves back just as I get my fingers around his massive bicep, but his momentum doesn't slow. His elbow connects with my face, sending me flat on my ass.

"Fuck." I cry out, my palms immediately moving to cover my nose as streams of red coat the once yellow bodice of my dress.

Hearing my wail of pain, Ryker halts his assault on Chad and turns to glance behind himself. Seeing my disheveled state, his eyes widen, and he pushes off Chad immediately. Chad wastes no time clambering off the asphalt and running away. Figures the loafer-wearing pussy wouldn't wait to check on me... one more reason I should have known better.

"Holy shit, Addison." He scrambles over to me, his palm presses into my back as he shifts me onto his lap. "Let me see." He jerks my hands down, revealing my now swollen nose. "Fuck. It doesn't look broken, but let's get you to the ER. Why in the hell would you get in between two men fighting?"

"Are you kidding me? Are you actually trying to make this my fault? How about why are you beating the shit out of a stranger?" I try to stand, but Ryker squeezes me against him and pushes us both off the pavement. "Put me down, you ogre."

"Ogre?" Ryker huffs a laugh. "Sweetheart, you need to relax. Give me your keys."

"Why would I do that?" I press my fingers to stave off the pounding headache building.

"I'm driving you home. You're in no condition to ride on the back of my motorcycle, so I'm driving *your* truck." Before I can argue, Ryker sets me down and snatches my purse. He jerks my keys free and latches onto my arm. "Let's go, *Princess*."

How in the hell did I go from getting drunk to push him out of my head to bleeding profusely and in his company? This night has turned into some kind of nightmare. And the worse part about it... my body still reacts to his presence.

Fucking great.

Filled with turmoil, I don't realize Ryker's put me on the passenger seat and shut the door. I watch through blurry eyes as he rounds the front of my truck and jerks open the driver's-side door. The truck hums with a gentle rhythm as I watch Ryker climb inside. His body fills the cab with tension and unspoken emotions. The truck's interior was cloaked in shadows, the dim glow of the dashboard lights revealing the lines of worry etched on his face. Ryker's strong hands tightly gripped the steering wheel, his knuckles whitening with the intensity of his emotions as he fights to contain them.

I know he's pissed, but at what, I'm not completely sure. He appeared out of no where and intervened, stepping in to protect me from a man who was most likely about to cross a line I couldn't stop. Now, we're sitting in silence, the weight of the encounter palpable. Ryker's features are etched with a mixture of concern and frustration, his broad shoulders tense as he wrestles with his emotions. Finally, unable to bear the weirdness inside the truck, I shift to the side and look at him.

"Why'd you do that, Ryker? I could've taken care of him myself. I wasn't about to leave with him."

"Are you fucking serious right now?" Ryker puts the truck in gear and eases out of the parking lot. "He had you cornered against the wall, Addison. One more step and he would've had you in the alley… then what? You think you could've fought him off while he tried to rape you?"

Sucking in a breath, I blink away the wetness gathering in my eyes. His words, while crass, are right. *Chad* wasn't someone I knew, and he could have easily overpowered me. Just thinking about what could've happened causes a burning in my chest as the reality settles hard over me. Turning my head, I glance out the window, wincing as pain snickers across my face.

"Shit, Addison." Ryker reaches out and grabs my hand. "I'm sorry. I hate that I hurt you. I was just trying to protect you, and I fucked that up."

Realizing we weren't heading in the direction of my hotel, I turn to look at him. "Where are we going?"

"My place."

Jerking in my seat, "What? I need to go to my hotel, Ryker."

"No." He flicks on the blinker and pulls down a long drive. "I need to look at your nose and I can bet you don't have a first-aid kit. Besides… when are you going to find a place to stay? You can't live in a hotel forever."

Shaking off the guilt his words cause, I shrug. "I don't know yet, but I'm sure the front desk has a first-aid kit."

He ignores my comment, so I sigh and glance out the windshield. The building that comes into view is not what I'm expecting. It's some kind of warehouse, making me wonder if he's really a serial killer about to 'off' me.

"A warehouse? You planning on murdering me and dumping my body out here? Seriously, Ryker. Why are we here?"

He kills the engine and smiles. "It's where I live."

Frozen to the spot, I barely register the sound as Ryker opens my door.

"You live in a warehouse?"

He snorts a laugh. "Come on, Addison. Let me get you inside, so I can get some ice on your face. You're already starting to bruise."

"Seriously, Ryker?" Easing out of the truck, I let him guide me to the front door. "This is your house?"

Ryker keys in some kind of code, resulting in an audible click. He pushes open the door and steps inside, tugging me behind his massive frame.

"Ryker, just take me home… this is ridicu—"

There is no hiding my shock. I'm greeted by an open and spacious living area that seamlessly blends industrial charm with a sleek, modern vibe. The high ceilings, exposed interior brick walls, and large windows that sit high off the floor give the space a sense of grandeur. I can't imagine what it looks like when the natural light floods the room during the day. A state-of-the-art kitchen with stainless steel appliances, set across from the expansive living room, is adorned with glossy black countertops, stainless steel fixtures, and ample storage space. The kitchen island, with its polished surface and stylish bar stools, helps create separation from the living area. To say I'm stunned speechless is an understatement. It isn't until Ryker chuckles that I move my gaze back to him.

"Not what you expected, is it?" He smirks, walking away from me toward the kitchen.

9

Ryker

THE MOMENT I saw that fucking tool of a guy pressing Addison into the wall, I turned into a raging bull. My mind blanked, and all I could see was her being hurt. Grabbing that douche canoe was nothing. I was ready to lay him out, but sweet Addison stepped in the way, and fuck if I didn't hit her.

Needing to ensure I take care of her, I all but forced her into the car. I wanted to turn her over my knee and paddle her sweet ass for putting herself in harm's way—and for drinking while she was alone. Now standing here in the entry of my house, I can't take my eyes off her.

I'm pretty sure she's eating her comments made about my place.

Her eyebrows arch gently upward, further emphasizing the sense of surprise etched across her face as her gaze scans the open expanse of the interior. Her eyes, initially filled with agitation, now hold a mix of disbelief and awe, as if the unexpected sight of where I call home pleases her. Fuck, if that doesn't cause a weird sensation in my chest.

"I owe you an apology." Addison stumbles slightly in the come-fuck-me heels she's wearing as she moves deeper into the room. "I really thought you were bringing me out to murder me." She snorts at her ridiculous words. "But this place is amazing. Not at all what I would expect for someone like you."

"Like me?" I pull open the freezer and grab a bag of frozen peas, watching as she sets her clutch down on the counter. "Not sure what that means, but come sit. I need to look at your face."

Addison ambles over to one of the stools tucked under the island. Dragging it out she plops down, her eyes watching me as I move toward her.

"I guess I should thank you for rescuing me... even though you fucked up my nose."

Wincing at her words, I sit down in front of her and drag her stool between my legs. Brushing her hair away from her face I press the frozen vegetables against her face. She tries to hide the wince, but she's not good at hiding the pain.

"I'm really sorry I did this, Addison. I didn't realize you were behind me... granted, I didn't think you'd jump into the fray."

"I shouldn't have grabbed you." Addison's eyes are nothing short of enchanting, and I faintly hear her words. "It was stupid."

"What was stupid?" I asked, blinking my confusion.

Addison smirks at my blatant miss of information. "Grabbing your arm. I shouldn't have done that."

Staring into her eyes, I notice a mixture of emotions playing across her face, revealing something akin to vulnerability. Her eyes flicker to my mouth as she swallows. Cupping her cheek in my palm, I brush my thumb across her lip, eliciting a hiss from her.

Lifting the peas from her nose, I drop it on the counter behind her.

"You still feeling the alcohol, or did the TKO move to your face sober you up?"

"A punch to the face did the trick." She smiles, wincing slightly from the pain.

My fingers gently trace the bruise forming around the bridge of her nose. Addison's eyes hold a glimmer of curiosity, drawing me in like a magnet. Her shoulders relax as her posture subtly leans toward me, a silent invitation for something we both crave but shouldn't want. It's as though I'm a ship being lured across the ocean by a siren's call, and I lean in to meet her halfway. As her lips part, I pause, wondering if I'm reading the moment right. Before I can discern what she wants, her mouth presses against mine, ending any doubt.

Momentarily struck by the shock of her warm lips, I freeze. When her lips part, my mind is hit with the all-consuming need to claim her. A simple flick of her tongue ignites the flames of passion, and I pull her closer. Addison's fingers are suddenly in my hair as she tightens her hold on me. Time stands still, and the world falls away, leaving only the exquisite and life-altering feel of her in my embrace.

Something snaps inside me, and I lift her off the seat, shifting her body to the island countertop. Placing myself between her thighs, the skirt of her dress gathers around the form fitting bodice, leaving her silky panties visible. Pressing my palm to her back, I move her closer, wedging my rock-hard cock against the tiny satin strip covering her core. Even through the fabric of my jeans, I can feel the heat of her desire. Addison whimpers as I grind my rock-hard shaft into the apex of her body.

Needing more, she bucks her hips, desperate to create some friction. My fingers find the hem of the yellow material covering her body. As I slip it over her head and toss it to the floor, the crimson drips splattering onto the floor catch my eyes.

Like a bucket of ice dumped on a raging inferno, I growl, "Fuck." As I step back slightly, Addison digs her nails into my forearms, desperate to keep me close.

"What?"

"Your nose is bleeding." Moving away from her body propped on the edge of the counter, "Don't move, Princess."

Hurrying to the cabinet over the sink, I pull down the first-aid kit I store inside in case of an emergency. The box looks more like something for fishing tackle, not medical supplies, but being a boxer, I've grown accustomed to keeping shit stocked everywhere—my house, car, and office—anywhere I might decide to spar. Since Addison and I got distracted, she hasn't seen the best room in the house... well, *second* best.

Addison is clutching her nose with her head tilted back when I move back between her knees. Despite the streaks of red marring her porcelain skin, my dick twitches at the sight of her in nothing but her satin bra, panties, and red high heels. Shaking off the sudden pulse of desire, I set the plastic container down and open the lid. Sifting through a few of the contents, I pull out a roll of cotton gauze, specifically sized for this type of injury.

"Let go of your face, babe." Addison drops her head, her hands slowly shifting away from her nose. Leaning forward, I carefully press the absorbent material into her nostril. "I know this feels weird, but it will staunch the flow of blood." I reach back into the box and snag a packet of wipes. Pulling out a moist towelette, I slowly wipe at her skin. "I'm so fucking sorry."

Her eyes glisten with an emotion I can't read, but desperate to understand.

"It's okay, Ryker. Really, it wasn't your fault. It was a stupid accident, but um… do you think maybe I could take a shower? I feel gross, not to mention embarrassed."

"Embarrassed?" I frown, not understanding what she could be embarrassed about.

"Yeah." She wiggles against the counter. "I'm sitting here on your counter nearly naked, and I bled on you when you attempted to kiss me."

"Attempted? Sweetheart, I'm pretty sure I kissed you just fine. And even covered in blood, you've got my dick ready to rip open my zipper." I step closer, pressing my very hard erection into her center. "Thinking about you in the shower makes it even harder."

"Oh." She bites her lip, her eyes glancing down at the bulge in my pants, and blinks. "So… can I shower?"

Hating to divest her of her sexy as fuck shoes, I pull them off and toss them onto the kitchen floor. I wrap my arms around her and lift her from the counter, laughing at the squeak she lets out.

"Yep, let's go get you cleaned. Maybe your nose will stop bleeding and we can pick up where we left off."

"Ryker I can walk." Addison wraps her legs around me, her arms tangling behind my neck. "I'll get blood on you this way."

"Guess that means I'll just need to shower, too." As careful as can be, I climb the spiral staircase and carry her down the hall to my bedroom. Stepping inside, I don't give her any time to take in the space and hurry into the enormous bathroom.

"Whoa." Her voice is barely above a whisper, but the admiration for the space is clear in her tone. "This is amazing."

"It's my second favorite room in the house." Easing her down on top of the vanity, I step back and flick on the shower.

"Second?" Her eyes scan the room, taking in every detail.

"I'll show you the first later." Smiling, I move in front of her. "Now, let's get you cleaned up."

Grabbing my shirt by the collar, I jerk it over my head. Her quick intake of breath makes my cock pulse. As I reach for the button on my jeans, she hops off the counter.

Folding her arms across her chest, she narrows her eyes at my movements. "What are you doing?"

Closing the distance between us, I carefully reach up and tug the cotton swab out of her nose. "See, it's stopped bleeding."

She closes her eyes and huffs. "You're avoiding my question. What. Are. You. Doing?"

Reaching around her back, I unclasp her bra and let it slip off her shoulders. Holding her gaze, I hook my thumb in her panties and jerk the flimsy material until it snaps. Tossing them out the door, I lick my lips and grin.

"You have about two seconds to say no, Addison."

"Ryker."

My name sounds more like a whimper, and it's all the approval I need before I drop to my knees and press my face between her legs.

"Ohmygod."

Her fingers dig into my shoulders as I drag my tongue between her silky folds. My hands wrap around her thighs, tugging her closer so I can eat her the way I want. Feeling her knees buckle as I tongue her center makes me smile against the tuft of blond hair above her clit. Pushing her legs apart with my shoulder, I move my fingers to her core. Adding a digit between her folds, I suckle her nub between my lips and bite down slightly.

Like a trigger to a bomb, she detonates. Her pussy convulses around my finger as her cream coats my knuckles. Moving my hand from between her legs, I firmly grip her hips and trail my lips up her firm belly to her small, but perfect tits. They're the perfect fit for my grasp, and I take full advantage of that fact by cupping them in my palm.

"You're fucking beautiful." I slam my lips over hers, kissing her.

Addison's mouth doesn't disappoint. She sucks the tip of my tongue into her mouth hard. Moaning against her lips, I drop my hands and quickly shove my pants and boxers off, kicking them to the side. Without detaching our lips, I slowly back our bodies up, guiding us into the shower. The massive enclosure has two large bench seats lining two of the walls. They're wide enough to lie down if I want to relax after a match, but the best feature is the multi-shower heads placed throughout the space.

The hot spray of the pulsating water soaks our bodies as our lips stay fused. Addison's hand moves south along my naked torso until her tiny fingers wrap around my engorged shaft. Jerking at the sensations of her grasp, I can't help but hiss.

"Shit, Princess... Touch me too much, and I'll fucking blow my load."

Addison cocks an eyebrow at me, smirking as she lowers herself to the tiled floor.

"What are you— Holy *fuck*."

Her lips wrap around my shaft as she expertly swallows my cock into her mouth. Her chestnut tendrils fall into her face as she glances up at me. I'm not a small guy, so she grasps my shaft at the base, jerking me off as she takes what she can into her throat. This girl is fucking obliterating me for any other woman. I don't know what to think as the thought assaults my conscience. Before she can get me off, I jerk her to her feet and spin her around.

"Hands on the wall and don't move." Stepping out of the shower, I jerk open the medicine cabinet and retrieve a condom. Ripping open the packet with my teeth, I sheath myself in the latex barrier and step back in behind her. "I'm going to fuck you hard and fast this time, Addison. You ready for me, Princess?"

She glances over her shoulder and smirks. "Show me what you've got, Ry."

Hearing the nickname from her lips set me off in ways I can't explain. Gripping the globe of her ass with one hand, I kick her feet apart and grip my dick in my other hand. Dragging my shaft between her backside, I tease her puckered hole with my tip.

"I'm going to take this one day, but right now, I need to be buried deep inside your sweet pussy." Slowly easing my cock into her center, I close my eyes and relish the way her walls wrap around my shaft like silk. "Goddamn, baby. I knew you'd feel like heaven."

10

Addison

I'VE OFFICIALLY LOST my mind.

But as Ryker guides his big dick into my needy center, I don't care. He fills me in a way I've never experienced, and for now, I need him to keep moving. Pressing my ass into him as a hint of what I want, Ryker begins to move behind me. My hands brace against the tiled surface as he rocks into me from behind.

"Fuck, Addison." His grunt of approval spurs me on, and I bounce against his thrust. "That's it, baby, fuck my dick. Jesus Christ, your pussy is sucking my cock like it doesn't want to let go. I've never felt anything like this." He pounds into me, his dirty words driving me wild. "I need to see your face."

He suddenly withdraws from my core and spins me around. As if I'm a mere rag doll, he lifts me with ease and presses me against the wall. With a quick adjustment of his stance, his shaft finds its way back inside me, and this time, the angle is so much better. I swear his cock is hitting the back of my uterus, but every stroke is like a match lighting a fire inside me.

The water cascades around us, giving an illusion of being beneath a waterfall as Ryker rams himself inside me over and over again. My hands press into the tiles as I arch my backside, silently demanding him to press himself deeper somehow. I'm pretty sure I'm going to have bruises on my hips from where he grips me, but I don't care—I'll wear them like a fucking badge of honor. Hell, maybe they'll match the one I'm sure is growing a deeper hue across my nose.

"You're close, Princess." His hand slips around my side and dips between my legs as his belly leans into my back, his cock still buried deep inside my womb. "I need you to come for me." Ryker presses his finger against my swollen nub, swirling it around the tender flesh. Desperate to get me off, he pinches my clit, triggering my orgasm. It's like a cataclysmic explosion deep inside me. Swirls of black fill my vision as I give into the coil of desire rushing through my veins.

"Ryker!" I scream out his name, my pussy spasming around his shaft as my walls practically choke his cock.

"Fuuuuuck." He growls through his orgasm as he powers into me from behind. His cock swells before expelling every drop into the rubber, stretching it to the max. "Goddamn, Addison." His hot breath mingles with the beads of water coating my spine. "I've gotta take care of the condom."

I muddle my way to the bench and slide down onto my ass, trying to catch my breath. Ryker stands outside the glass enclosure, disposing of the condom. I watch in confusion as he turns and braces himself against the sink with his head bowed. Concern washes over me when he doesn't speak.

"Ryker?" I call out his name, unsure about what he's doing. When he doesn't answer, I call out again. "Ryker, you coming back in?"

Without a single word muttered, he turns and walks from the bathroom, leaving me to stare at the empty doorway. Blinking in confusion, I don't move from my spot, unsure of what just happened. *Where the hell did he go?*

After a few moments, Ryker still hasn't come back, so I stand and quickly rinse my body. Cutting the water off, I step from the massive enclosure onto the plush gray floor mat and grab a towel from the hanging bar. Drying off, I squeeze the water from my hair and wrap the soft cotton around my body. Using the edge of my hand, I wipe away the fog covering the glass and stare at my reflection. My eyes are cocooned in a slight purple hue, evidence of the earlier mishap that led us to this moment. Inhaling, I let the air fill my lungs before blowing it out again. Ryker is completely MIA, sending me the message he thinks what we just did in the shower is an epic mistake.

Glancing down at the floor, I scoop my bra off the floor, my panties nowhere in sight. I inhale, fortifying my nerves, and open the door. Part of me is relieved Ryker isn't in the bedroom. The other part of me is pissed as hell. Not wanting to spend another second in his house, I grab his discarded t-shirt and slip it on. The thought of doing the walk of shame in just a shirt makes my skin crawl, but I know my dress is no longer wearable.

Easing open the door, I pause, listening for any sign Ryker is nearby. I can faintly hear sounds coming from downstairs. The staircase, something I didn't pay attention to earlier, is absolutely beautiful. It's mostly metal with wood planks for steps that wind down into the living space. Scanning the open floor plan, Ryker isn't there. Hearing soft music coming from behind where we came in from the garage, I tiptoe down the hallway and stop in front of a door.

Needing to get seeing him over with, I open the door and gasp. The space is bigger than I expect, but what draws my eyes in is the man pounding the hanging bag in the corner. Obviously, Ryker takes his training seriously because he has an entire gym in his home. Standing in the doorway, I hesitate to interrupt, but we need to talk.

Ryker must see me out of the corner of his vision because he stops mid-swing and grabs the bag, so it stills. I start to speak, but stop, unsure of what to say to him. He shakes his head and lets go of the bag.

"What's wrong, Addison?"

Shocked by the dripping sarcasm lacing his tone, I clench my fists to quell the anger and step into the room.

"What's wrong?" I narrow my gaze at him and through clenched teeth mutter, "What's wrong, *Ryker*, is you left me alone after what we did in the shower."

"So what, Addison? We fucked. That doesn't mean shit to me. You wanted my dick, and I wanted to give it to you. We did that, and now you can go."

Tears bit at the back of my eyelids, threatening to fall—something I absolutely refuse to do.

"Are you serious? So... what? I'm just another notch on your fucking bedpost?"

"Did you think this was going to be something more?" he smirks.

"Fuck you, Ryker. I didn't ask you to bring me here—and I sure as shit didn't ask you *save* me tonight." I start toward the door and pause when he speaks.

"Jesus, Addison. You act like you're something special. You're not. We fucked, that's it. Get over yourself, *Princess.*"

Turning to look at him, I can't stop the teardrop from rolling down my cheek.

"Wow. Get over myself? Really, Ryker? I thought you were different… guess you're just another selfish bastard." I step through the open door and pause. Glancing over my shoulder, "And I quit. Fuck you and your gym, *Saint*." His nickname spills out with venom as I walk out.

I head into the kitchen, desperate to get the fuck out of his house as his words burn into my psyche. Words I've heard before from a man. Grabbing my discarded shoes off the floor, I snatch my purse from the bar top and dig my keys out from the bottom. I'm probably still not in any condition to drive, but I don't care—I'll risk it to get away from him. I pause at the front door, looking back down the hall that leads to his gym.

Ryker isn't the kind of guy who cares about women, not when he can have whoever he wants. I wish I was one of those women who could just see him as a score, but the ache in my chest reminds me I'm not. And for the life of me, I don't know why. It's not like he's been nice to me in the two weeks I've been working for him. When he stepped in and pummeled that dickhead's face tonight, I saw a side of him I thought proved he was a decent guy.

Moving to the front door, I stare at the keypad beside it, reality sinking in. Of course, the damn thing doesn't open like a normal person's front entry. Silently praying for it to be unlocked, I grip the handle and tug. *Fuck*. It's locked, and I have no clue how to get out. Pressing my head against the cool metal door, I drop what I'm holding onto the floor and suck in a breath. I refuse to go back into the gym and ask him to let me out of this hellhole. It's humiliating enough that he dismissed me with such little care. Asking him to let me out is the icing on this shitty night.

Spinning on my heel, I close my eyes and take a deep breath. I don't want to be here—and he doesn't want me here, but I can't get out of this hellhole. Glancing around, I spot a small bathroom off the hallway, and though it's near his gym, I hurry over and lock myself inside. The room is bigger than most half-bathrooms, for which I'm grateful. I move over to the sink and stare at myself in the mirror, wincing once more at the monster staring back.

As I continue to look at myself, the tears begin to fall. *How did I get here?* Moving against the wall opposite the door, I slide down, sitting between the toilet and the cabinet. Drawing my knees up to my chest, I wrap my arms around my legs and let the tears fall.

There's no coming back from this. I lied to get close to him, and now, I've fucked up and stand no chance at salvaging why I'm here to begin with. My dignity and job are royally fucked. When I finally figure out how to get out of this fucking prison, I'll call my boss and resign. There's no other option. I didn't close the case.

Fuck.

How did I expect to close this case... when I couldn't even close my legs?

11

Ryker

As I hit the bag, all I can think about is Addison. I've never allowed myself to get close to a woman, but what we just did in the shower obliterated my walls—and that scares the fuck out of me. I had to get out of there, put distance between us.

Hearing the door open, I cut my eyes to the woman who has me all tangled up inside.

"What do you want, Addison?" I don't mean for the words to bite, but that's exactly what they do.

"What's wrong?" Addison narrows her gaze at me as her jaw tenses. "What's wrong, *Ryker*, is you left me alone after what we did in the shower."

Needing to put my walls back in place, I channel the asshole inside, but as soon as the words leave my mouth, I regret them.

"So what, Addison. We fucked. That doesn't mean shit to me. You wanted my dick, and I wanted to give it to you. We did that, and now you can go."

I watch as her eyes sparkle with unabashed tears and a part of me wants to take the words back, but I don't.

"Are you serious? So… what? I'm just another notch on you fucking bedpost?"

"Did you think this was going to be something more?" I smirk.

"Fuck you, Ryker. I didn't ask you to bring me here—and I sure as shit didn't ask you *save* me tonight." She starts toward the door, but my words stop her.

"Jesus, Addison. You act like you're something special. You're not. We fucked, that's it. Get over yourself, *Princess.*"

It nearly guts me as a fat tear drop rolls down her cheek.

"Wow. Get over myself. Really, Ryker? I thought you were different… guess not." She steps through the open door and pauses. I'm not expecting her next words. "And I quit. Fuck you and your gym, *Saint.*"

I'm a complete fucking dick.

I should go after her, tell her I'm a fucking idiot, but I remain rooted to the floor. The feelings she stirs in me scare the shit out of me. Instead of facing them, I do the complete opposite. I shut them down and lash out at the one woman I actually want.

Fuck.

Rage courses through my veins and I let my fist fly, needing to expel the frustration burning inside my chest, but trying to push her from my head does the opposite. A replay of what we shared in the shower is on constant repeat in my head, and no matter how hard I hit the fucking bag, her scent, her taste, hell, the way her fucking moans sound, echo inside my brain. After nearly exhausting myself, I grab the bag and hold on as I catch my breath. I toss the gloves to the floor and grab a towel off the bench. Wiping down the sweat from my body, I suddenly freeze when a thought hits me.

The fucking door.

There's no way she can get out of my house. Not without the code to open the door. *Shit.* I toss the towel down and stride out the gym door. Going into the kitchen I find her dress still on the floor, right where we left it. Her shoes are gone, as is her purse, which confuses me, knowing she still has to be inside. Moving into the living room, I scan the open space, still lost as to where she's hiding. I don't miss the fact her shoes and bag are still at the door. Picking them up off the floor, I spin in a circle and pause.

Where the hell are you, Princess?

As I start toward the steps, I hear a sound from the hall leading toward the gym. It doesn't take me long to figure out it's Addison. She's inside the half-bathroom. Stepping up to the door I raise my hand to knock when I hear a sound that nearly takes me to my knees. Closing my eyes, I press my palms against the door.

"Addison?" Her sobs continue, ripping at the very fiber of my soul. "Baby… let me in."

"Fu-ck you… R-Ryker." Her words are garbled as she continues to cry. "J-Just l-leave mm-ee alone."

"Let me in, please." I press my head against the wood. "I'm sorry for what I said."

When she doesn't answer me, I try the knob, knowing it's probably locked. Fortunately for me, my doors can all be opened with a special key. Leaving the door, I head into the kitchen and pull out the pin key from a drawer and hurry back to the bathroom.

"Addison… honey, open the door." When I still get no response, I push the thin metal into the hole, pleased when I hear the lock disengage. Setting the key on the top of the door, I twist the knob and slowly open the door, careful not to hit her with it.

What I find knocks the air out of my lungs. Addison has her knees drawn to her chest, and her sobs cause her body to shake almost violently.

"Fuck…" I squat in front of her and reach out, pressing my hands to her knees. "Jesus, I did this to you. Come on, Addison. Let me get you out of here."

"I j-just w-w-want to go home." She whimpers, burying her head further into her folded arms.

"I can't let you do that, Princess. Not until I fix what I fucked up."

Ignoring my words, she draws her feet closer to her body. Refusing to allow her to sit huddled up in the bathroom, I slide my hands beneath her legs and scoop her into my arms. She's so distraught, she doesn't realize when I lift her from the floor. Cradling her against my body, I navigate us out of the tiny space. Climbing the steps, I carry her straight into my bedroom.

As soon as I lay her down, Addison pries her eyes open.

"I don't want to be here."

"To fucking bad, Addison. I fucked up and said some things I didn't mean. You didn't deserve them and for that, I'm sorry. You're in no condition to drive home, so thank God you couldn't get out of my house. I'd never forgive myself if something had happened to you."

"I doubt that," she whispers, rolling away from me. "I'm nothing special, remember?"

"The problem is you are special, Addison." Reaching out, I press my hand against her back, noticing she's in one of my t-shirts. "And it scares the fuck out of me."

"Please stop, Ryker." She jerks away from me, causing my hand to drop away from her body. "Since you won't let me leave, at least leave me alone."

Stuck between wanting to give her what she wants, and not wanting to leave, I sigh. I want to make her see what I said was lies, but it's obvious I fucked things up so much, she isn't interested in hearing my apology.

"Fine, I'll let you sleep, but tomorrow we're going to talk, Addison."

I pull the blanket over her body and push to my feet. Her back is still to me, and I can't help but stand there and stare. Her chestnut brown hair is fanned out over my pillow, and I'm hit with a vision of waking up to her like this every day. Shaking the wishful thoughts from my head, I turn and leave the room. I'll give her a little while to fall asleep before I climb into bed with her—I'm not sleeping on my couch.

Ambling down the stairwell, I head into the kitchen, jerk open the refrigerator, and grab a beer. Twisting off the top, I press the bottle to my lips and drag the amber liquid into my mouth. The coolness as it slides down my throat quells some of the disgust I'm feeling.

My mother would be disgusted with me, knowing how I treat women—Addison in particular. Closing my eyes, I conjure an image of my mom and smile. She was everything to my brothers and me. Byron filled a void when my dad died, but losing him still hurt. Sure, my grandfather was still alive then, but he wasn't a man who showed much compassion—and I think his personality rubbed off on me. After what landed me in jail, I came out a different man.

Bitter and distrusting of everyone who wasn't already in my inner circle.

That includes the woman upstairs in my bed. Only she doesn't deserve it, and the guilt I'm feeling threatens to pull me under. Tossing the empty bottle into the trashcan, I navigate back up the stairs and stop outside my door. Keeping Addison at arm's length is the right thing to do but not by causing tears.

Pushing inside the room, I tiptoe to the edge of the bed. "Addison," I whisper into the quiet room, waiting to see if she's still awake. As I watch her chest rise and fall, I breathe out a sigh of relief, knowing she's knocked out. Shoving off my shorts, I tug down the covers and slip in beside her. Hesitating for only a second, I pull her body against mine, needing the closeness even if I don't deserve it.

"I'm sorry, Princess. You're doing something to me I don't know what to do with. But you didn't deserve my hateful words. Sleep sweet girl. I've got you now."

The heat of her body felt perfect nestled against my body. The steady rise and fall of her breath is like a rhythmic beat that would normally lull me to sleep, but not tonight. Tonight, my thoughts pollute my subconscious in a way that demands I stay awake. Feeling her tucked against me is pure torture in ways I didn't prepare myself for. A feeling of panic stirs inside me, threatening to make me run again, but I hold her despite my fears.

At some point, I must doze off because I wake to the feeling of weight against my chest. I've rolled over to my back, opening myself up for Addison to shift her position as well. Her hair is draped over my shoulder like melted chocolate, with her head tucked perfectly in the crook of my arm. Her arm is laid across my body, her fingers splayed against my chest. Her right leg is tucked between my legs, putting her bare pussy against my leg. The heat of her core radiates like an inferno, which wakes my cock up. Trying to shift out from under her, she wakes up, her eyes widen with shock at our position.

"What the fuck, Ryker? Why are we in bed together?"

"I put you to sleep last night, Addison. I fucked up and hurt you, but I wasn't about to let you stay in the goddamn bathroom."

She leans up, looking at my face. "That doesn't explain why you're in bed with me."

"I needed to sleep."

She shifts, realizing she's not wearing any panties and is pressed against my thigh. "Fuck." Her body stills as her eyes squeeze closed.

"Addison." I cup her cheek. "I didn't mean the things I said. I was scared and lashed out at you."

"Scared? Bullshit, Ryker. You got what you wanted and needed me to leave."

Flipping her over to her back, I pin her beneath me.

"Look at me, Addison." Her eyes shift to meet mine. "You're not a notch. I didn't know how to handle what I'm feeling."

"I don't need you to patronize me, Ryker. Just let me up so I can leave. We can forget about everything."

"I'm not forgetting shit." My cock twitches against her core. "Tell me you didn't like what we did, Addison. Tell me your body didn't fit perfectly with mine as I slipped my cock between your folds."

"Ryker." She whimpers, shifting her body beneath me.

The movement only succeeds in putting my dick in perfect position with her opening, and I can't hold back as I push inside her.

"Fuck, Princess."

"Don't do this, Ryker."

"Tell me to stop," I whisper, easing my shaft out and pushing it back in. "Tell me, Addison, and I'll pull out and walk away."

She clenches her eyes closed as her mouth opens, but instead of telling me to stop, a moan slips free, and I completely fucking lose it. My hips piston between her legs as I pound into her opening like a man possessed.

"God, your pussy was made for me." She digs her claws into my shoulders as her body bends underneath me. The slick feel of her walls wrapping around my shaft pushes me faster than I want. "Need you to cum, baby girl."

Sliding my palm between us, I pinch her swollen nub between my fingers. Addison cries out, her pussy gripping hold of my dick almost painfully. I pump two more times and empty my load inside her. As I pull out, I realize my fuck up immediately.

"Fuck." I roll off her and push off the bed. "This was a mistake."

Addison opens her eyes, which immediately fill with tears. "Unlock your fucking door."

She scrambles up, practically running out of the room.

"Addison… wait." I race after her, slipping down the last two steps as I land at the base. She's grabbed all her things and is pacing by the door.

"Open it up. *Now*."

"Addison… let me explain." I walk toward her, but she holds up her hand.

"No… I don't want to listen to anything you have to say. I'm stupid for letting that happen, but I'm done. Open the door, *please.*"

Seeing I'm not going to get through, I step around her and key in the code. As soon as the door unlocks, she snatches it open and ducks under my arm to exit.

"Addison, it's not what you think."

"Fuck you, Ryker." Her eyes well with tears as she runs down the steps and hurriedly climbs into her truck.

I don't miss the tear drop that rolls down her cheek as she turns on the engine. As she backs the truck up and shifts it into drive, I see her glance in the rearview mirror. The look of utter devastation punches me right in the gut, and I can't move. I stand on my stoop watching until her taillights disappear down my long drive.

I don't know how long I stand there like a lost little boy, staring at the emptiness, but finally, pressing my hand to my chest to stave the pain pounding inside me, I turn and walk into my house.

I thought losing my professional career broke my heart, but I was wrong.

Addison just drove away with my heart… and she doesn't even know it.

12

Addison

I LAY CURLED on my side staring at the wall. Thoughts of the last two days swirl like a black hole, threatening to pull me under. I've avoided all calls from my employer, my best friend, and most of all, Ryker. Knowing there's only one thing to do, I peel myself out of the bed and force myself to shower.

Once I pull myself together enough to be seen in public, I grab my bag and head down to the parking garage. Climbing into my truck, all I can think about is the last time I was inside the damn thing... with Ryker. Huffing out a frustrated breath, I drive out of the parking garage and navigate toward the gym. Seeing Ryker is going to be painful, but I brought it on myself.

Pulling into the parking lot, I park and cut off the engine. I can't bring myself to get out as I stare out the windshield at Strykers. I don't know how long I sit there, but I nearly shit myself when there's a tap on the window. Glancing to my side, I spot Luke standing at my door. He motions for me to roll down the glass, but I push open the door instead.

"Addi." I can't help but smile at the use of my nickname. Unlike Ryker, he calls me by the shortened version of my name. "Ryker said you've been sick. You feeling better?"

"What?" I'm caught off guard by his statement. "Ryker said I was sick?"

"Yeah… were you not?" His brows furrow in confusion. "I thought maybe that's why you were just sitting here… thought you might still feel bad."

"Oh." I swallow down my confusion and force a smile. "Right… sure. I was sick. But I'm better now. Is Ryker here?"

"Yeah." Luke nods his head. "Inside." He steps to the side, letting me climb out, then shuts my door for me. "I'll warn you though… he's been in a real shit mood."

"Great," I mumble as I follow him inside.

I'm immediately hit with the sounds of vinyl against flesh, the sound drawing my eyes to the center ring. A man who appears to be a few inches shorter than Ryker is bouncing around the soft surface. His lithe body is covered in tattoos, but it only adds to his allure. Don't get me wrong, he has a swimmer's style body with layers of ripped muscle covering the upper half. His hair is blonde, shaved on the sides, giving him the appearance of having a mohawk without the ends sticking up. When his face turns toward me, despite the protective helmet covering his head, I realize the man is Axel, a new boxer Ryker's been training.

As he moves to the side, I gasp when his opponent comes into view. I've seen Ryker spar, but I've never seen him like this. The fury rolling off him hits me like waves on a turbulent sea, and I instinctively step back, bumping into Luke.

Luke eyes me speculatively. "You good?"

"Yeah, but is he?" I tilt my head in the direction of Ryker and Axel.

Luke simply shrugs. "Told you he's been in a shit mood. Axel knew what he was getting into when he stepped into the ring today."

Turning back to the brutal workout, my eyes stay glued to the man I want to hate. There is no doubt in my mind Ryker is still a god in the ring, making me wonder why he never went back to his life before being incarcerated. Each time his glove brushes against Axel's flesh, I swear I can feel his sweat rolling down his skin. Their bodies spin, putting Axel's back to me and an up-close view of Ryker's front. Which means I'm in his line of sight.

It's like a slow-motion train wreck coming at me, and there's nothing I can do to stop it. Ryker's gaze lands on me, and he falters, giving Axel the opportunity he needs. His long arm reaches out, connecting with the side of Ryker's padded head. A look of shock passes over his expression as his face contorts from the powerful punch. My eyes widen, and I vaguely hear Luke holler his name as Ryker topples to the side. My brain registers the noise his massive frame makes hitting the floor of the ring like a head-on collision. The imaginary vibration I feel jolts through me, sparking my feet forward, and I practically leap into the ring without thinking about it.

Axel drops beside him, but my hands are the first ones on his helmet.

"Ryker." I try to tamp down the panic as I feel around for the latch holding the padded protection in place.

"Hey." Axel strips off his gloves and presses his bare hand over mine. "Addi, let me help him." He turns back to Luke. "Luke, get her out of here."

"Let Axel deal with him, Addi." Luke grabs me under my arms and drags me out. "He's fine, I promise. He just got his bell rung."

As Luke stands me up, I notice Ryker sitting up and stripping off his gear. Embarrassment about letting him catch me staring has me ducking my head and letting Luke lead me to Ryker's office. Pushing inside, he directs me to the leather couch against the wall.

"Sit there." He goes to the mini-fridge in Rykers' office and grabs water. "Drink this."

Snatching the bottle from his hand I uncap the water and let the ice-cold liquid wash down my throat. "Thanks."

"What the hell happened out there, Addi? You've been here long enough to know that shit happens in the ring when boxers are sparing. If Axel hadn't noticed you'd jumped in there, you could have been hurt."

"I don't know. I just freaked out. I thought…" My voice dies on my tongue as Ryker steps into the room. His eyes immediately land on me, and I can't help sucking in a breath.

"You good?" Luke looks up as he moves toward his desk.

"Yeah. Luke, can you give us a minute?" He glances at me, and I want to crawl beneath the cushions.

"Um… sure." Luke furrows his brows as he looks between the two of us. "Everything okay?"

"I just need a moment with Miss Quincy," Ryker assures, dipping his chin in response.

Startled by the use of my last name, Luke pauses. "Addi?"

It's weird hearing the concern in Luke's voice, seeing he hasn't been my biggest fan.

"It's fine, Luke. Thanks for the water and well…" I shrug, unsure of what to say.

"Let me know if you need something." He steps out, and I watch as Ryker closes and locks the door.

Ryker, dressed only in a pair of athletic shorts, moves to sit on the top of his desk. His palms press into the top, and his fingers grip the edge so tightly, his knuckles whiten. I look anywhere but at him, my nerves ricocheting through my body like an electrical storm brewing on the horizon.

"Look at me." Ryker's deep voice jolts me from my avoidance, and my gaze snaps to his. "Why are you here?"

Swallowing, I pinch my lips together, not sure of my answer.

"I don't know. Well… that's not true. I thought I knew why I was here, but now I'm not sure."

"You left my house, Addi."

"No shit, Ryker." My face scrunches in disgust. "You said what we did was a mistake, and you're right. I shouldn't have allowed what happened that morning to happen. Not after the way you treated me less than twelve hours earlier."

"No… you misunderstood, Addison, but you ran out of there before I could clarify what I said."

Confusion muddles my thoughts, but I shake my head in disagreement. "I didn't misunderstand anything."

Ryker narrows his gaze on me. "I was sincere when I apologized for my abhorrent behavior that night. And while you might have been right about me being selfish,"—he pushes off the desk and stalks toward me—"you're wrong about why I said it was a mistake." His body hovers over me, his arms caging me as I lean against the back of the couch, away from him.

"I've never brought a woman to my house, Addison. I've never let a woman into my bed. And I sure as shit have never fucked a woman without gloving up." He presses his knee between my legs. "But I did that with you."

My eyes suddenly widen in shock at the intensity of his words. "Wait—"

"Yeah, Princess. When I fucked you that morning, I wasn't wearing a condom. I got so lost in your body, I forgot the most important thing—to wrap my dick up. When I realized what I'd done, I said the first thing that popped into my head."

"That it was a mistake," I whisper, my heart pounding like a damn herd of elephants racing across the savanna. "I-I just assumed—"

"Yeah, assumed," he cuts me off. "You thought I meant what we did was a mistake. Addison." He reaches up and cups my cheek. The pad of his thumb brushes across my lip. "The only mistake happened the night before. The way I made you feel, that was an epic failure on my part. But darling,"—he leans so his lips are a breath away—"you've bewitched me. I seem to lose all sense when you're around. Axel's sucker shot is proof of that. I don't go down with one hit."

He doesn't let me get a word out before his lips cover mine. Like a moth to a flame, I don't fight it. I'm a glutton for punishment with this man, but the way he makes my body come alive is unlike anything I've ever felt. His touch ignites desire inside my body to a level I never knew existed between two people.

Even though I know being with him is on borrowed time, I'll risk the flames, even if it means risking a nuclear detonation when the clock stops ticking on what's between us.

13

Ryker

SLIPPING my fingers beneath the hem of Addison's t-shirt, I drag it over her head and toss it to the floor. Her eyes hold a hint of concern as I scan her body. I assume she thinks I'm disappointed in what she's wearing, but it's quite the contrary. She's sexy as fuck in a lace bra, but seeing her in a sports bra ignites a fire in my veins. A slight growl rumbles up from my chest from the squeak she emits when I scoop her off the couch and carry her to my desk. With a quick swipe of my arm, the contents covering the surface clatter to the floor, leaving the space to do whatever I please with her body.

"Ryker," Addison whispers as her fingers lace through the brown locks covering my head, holding my face still. "We shouldn't do this."

"I won't force you." I hold her gaze. "But I know you feel this thing between us. We're like fire and gasoline, Princess, and right now, I want to burn with you. Forget about everything else, and let me make you feel good."

I know she thinks she should say no, but cockiness spreads through me when her head bobs yes at what we both need. Gripping the elastic waist of her leggings, I pause, silently asking for permission. When she lifts her ass, giving me the room to pull the material down, along with her panties, my cock swells beneath the flimsy material covering it. I pause long enough to pull off her shoes but don't waste a second more and divest her of the material in my way.

She's completely naked now and watching me with apt attention as I push her legs apart and bend forward. I blow a puff of air against her aching center, and I smile when she hisses in pleasure. My gaze moves up to her face as a smirk covers mine. With a swift slap, I pop my hand against her wet pussy, making her jump.

"What the fuck, Ry—" Her words become a moan as my tongue plunges between her slick folds.

"Fuck, Princess. You've coated my desk in your sweet essence."

I dive back in, suckling the tender flesh, only this time, I add a finger. The pulsing motion I make inside her has her racing once more to the finish line as her pussy sucks my digit in and clamps down.

"Ryker." She cries out my name as her walls vibrate against my finger. The pulses rush throughout her entire body, rendering her languid in my hold. Collapsing on my desk, she lays limp.

I know she thinks there's no way I can make her cum again, but I'm not a man who quits until I get what I want. Rising from my perch between her creamy thighs, I wipe my mouth with the back of my arm. Through hooded eyes, Addison watches as I push my shorts down, freeing my shaft. I swear my dick has grown since the last time it was inside her, but she's good and ready for me.

How the hell does this woman do this to me?

Not even an hour ago, I thought she was ready to write me off. Now, I have her spread eagle on my desk, waiting for me to plunge my monster cock into her. I don't give Addison a chance to second guess the epic mistake she thinks we're making as I step forward and push inside her waiting channel. My fingers grip her legs so tight, I'm worried I'm hurting her, but looking at her lustful gaze, I figure the pain only heightens the sensation of my shaft moving inside her warm center. When I catch her gaze, I note her eyes are dilated, and she has a look of complete captivity.

As I thrust into her, the friction builds between us. Addison forces her hips up in a tango she knows will lead to relief. I can feel the orgasm pushing forward as my ball tightened, but I needed her to cum again. Lifting her leg to my shoulder, I slip my fingers to where we're joined and press into the swollen bud. Swirling my finger around in the slickness coating her core, I give her clit a quick pinch. That's all it takes for Addison to clamp down on my dick. Her inner walls tighten around my cock as she closes her eyes and chants my name over and over.

For a moment, it's as if I'm back in the ring, and fans are calling out my name, waiting for the knockout. As I pump into her, the muscles in my neck cord and the veins swell, nearly exploding as my release bursts free. A few more thrusts and I spill my seed inside her, coating her walls, marking her as mine. *Yeah... I didn't glove up again.* This time, I smile as the cum drips out of her pussy when I pull my dick out of her. Something about seeing my semen drip from her hole sets off something primal inside me.

Our bodies are slick with sweat as I step back. My heart beats out of control inside my chest, but I love the way it makes me feel. Leaving her spread out on my desk, I jerk up my shorts and duck into the bathroom. Wetting a towel, I walk out to find her in a pool of sated flesh on the wooden surface. Pausing between her legs, I wipe the moistened towel across her tender folds. Addison glances up, shock mirroring in her eyes at my motions.

I know she thinks this was just fucking, but it wasn't. I'm not sure if I'm ready to admit it, but what we just did was so much more—and that scares the fuck out of me. Handing her the towel, I walk to my mini-fridge and pull out another bottle of water. Uncapping it, I drink the entire contents. By the time I turn around, Addison has her clothes pulled back on.

"You need another water?"

"Uh… no thanks." She clasps her hands in front of her, shifting nervously on her feet. "Ryker… I don't—"

I rush in front of her and press my fingers over her lips.

"Don't." I press my lips to her forehead. "We seem to fuck things up after, so let's just not say something that will start a fight. I like you, Addison. And this,"—I drag my finger down her front—"thing between us makes me want to see where it can go."

"I don't know." She bites down on her bottom lip. "I won't deny we have some wicked sexual chemistry, but you don't do relationships. You said so yourself. And, although we've… well, ah,"—her eyes close for a minute—"had sex several times, this isn't me. I don't just fall into bed with men. I can't do casual or fuck buddies or whatever you want because my heart is always the one to take the beating when it ends."

"Fuck buddies?" I snort. "Addison, I've never asked you to be my fuck buddy. Granted, I've not been really clear about what we are, but this,"—I motion between us again—"is anything but casual. I've made some mistakes, and for whatever reason, you've come back. This time, I'm not going to fuck it up on purpose."

She takes a deep breath. "Are you forgetting I quit?"

"I didn't accept your resignation, hence the reason Luke thought you were out sick."

"Presumptuous of you, don't you think?" she asks, folding her arms across her chest.

"Hopeful, not presumptuous." I press my lips against hers. "Will you give it a chance?"

I watch as a myriad of emotions cross her face. I'm not sure what to make of them, but I don't care right now—as long as she says yes. Staring straight into my eyes, Addison smiles, and I swear it's like the sun is shining inside my office. As she opens her mouth to speak, a knock resounds on my door.

"Ryker." Luke's voice seeps through the wood.

Addison turns her head toward the door. "You should get that."

Narrowing my gaze on her, I step around her and open the door. "What?" I bark, making his eyebrows shoot up to his hairline.

"Um... sorry to interrupt, but you need to come out front. You, um... have a visitor you'll want to see."

I turn toward Addison. "Wait for me?" I cock my head, silently begging her with my eyes. "This conversation isn't done, Princess."

Glancing between me and Luke, she blows out a sigh. "Yeah... I'll wait for you."

Moving in front of her, I pull her against my chest and claim her lips. "I'll be back."

Luke stands slack jaw as I walk out into the hall. When he steps out, I glance back at her and notice the shocked expression from me claiming her in front of my closest friend. Winking, I pull the door shut as I turn to look at my best friend.

"I take it you and she are fucking?" Luke's expression morphs into one of irritation.

"We're seeing where the relationship might go. So, no, we're not *just* fucking, Luke. And I expect you to treat her with some respect. Addison is different. She isn't into me because I'm the Saint. She sees me—Ryker. Honestly, it scares the shit out of me, but I'm not willing to fuck it up again."

"Again?" He walks in step with me. "Do I even want to know?"

"No." I laugh as my head shakes with my response.

As I round the corner, I stop dead in my tracks.

"What the fuck are you doing here?" I cut my eyes over at my friend for not warning me of *who* the visitor waiting for me was.

He simply shrugs and I turn my eyes back to a man who helped make my life hell.

"Figured it was time to collect what you owe me, Ryker... or should I call you *Saint*?"

Luke presses his palm to my shoulder. "You want me to call Griffyn?"

"No, not yet." Turning my eyes back to the man I hoped I'd never see again, I clench my fists at my side. "You have some fucking nerve showing up here."

"I would think you would want to clear the air."

"Clear the air?" The thick Russian accent grates my nerves, and it takes every ounce of willpower not to lay this motherfucker on the ground. "Your boss wanted to win a fight by cheating. I'm sorry it led to your fighter's death, but it wasn't my fault. That lies solely with you and your fucked-up organization."

"You're a smart man, Ryker. In this business, it's a life for a life, and since you evaded death in lockup… well, we'll need to come up with another solution."

"Another solution?" I snort. "Do you hear yourself, Andrei? You didn't own me then… and you don't own me now. Turn around and get the fuck out of my gym, or you're liable to wind up like Gurin."

"Is that a threat?" Andrei steps forward, causing Luke to tense up.

Placing my hand on his chest, I shake my head no. "Take it as you want, Andrei, but I'm not getting in bed with you. Not now, not ever. So, go back and tell Aleski to fuck off. It's been a year since everything went down. Let the past stay in the past."

"See, Ryker, that's where you're wrong. We *don't* forget. And we'll get what we want from you. Your family isn't impervious to us. Remember that."

"You motherfucker. You stay away from my family. They don't have anything to do with this, nor can they give you what you want. Get out before I call the cops." I try to stifle the rage burning inside me as Andrei stares me down. If he thinks my family is a weakness, he doesn't know my brothers or my sister, for that matter. They're just as crazy as me and won't let some goons intimidate them.

"Oh… um, Ryker." Addison steps beside me, her eyes moving between me and the man, obviously out of place in a suit. "I'm going to head home for now. We can talk later… or tomorrow when I come in to work."

"I asked you to stay in my office, Addison." I keep my eyes on Andrei as I speak the words.

She steps up to my chest, gripping my chin in her fingers.

"And I didn't listen to you. I've got things I need to do, and waiting was taking forever." She stands on her tiptoes and brushes her lips across mine. "Call me later." She glances over at Luke. "Luke... see you tomorrow."

I watch as she moves around Andrei and out the entrance. I don't miss the way his eyes follow her, nor do I miss the smirk when he turns back to face us.

"Looks like you have another weakness. We'll be in touch, Ryker. Soon."

"Fuck."

"Yeah, you can say that again." I close my eyes and take several breaths to calm myself. "What the fuck does Aleski want with me?"

Logan shrugs. "More importantly... you just painted a target on your girl's back. Maybe you should back off."

"Not happening, Luke. I'm not walking away again because if I do, I'll lose her for good." I fist my hair and scream. "Fuck."

Addison

I'M A FUCKING WEAK WOMAN. I came here to tell Ryker who I really am and wound up flat on my back—*again*. It's not as if he treats me like I probably deserve. Hell, the opposite, in fact. But there's something about him that draws me in when I'm near him. Pacing the office, I wrestle with what to do now.

He has no idea why I actually came here, and it's killing me to keep it from him. There's no doubt in my mind when he learns I'm an attorney and have been lying about what I do, he's going to hate me. I have only two more weeks to get him to come to Atlanta for the meeting with the firm. I could just tell him here, but the firm insists on a sit-down with everyone affected. I'm starting to realize why they haven't pushed the matter. It's going to blow up a lot of people's lives... and now mine is at risk of being hurt.

Lifting my bag off the ground, I rifle through it and pull out the file I've carried around since arriving in Nashville. Flipping through the contents, I cringe. *Why did I volunteer for this?* Shoving the ticking time bomb back into my purse, I set it down and grab my shoes to tug them on. Ryker asked me to wait, but he's been out there forever. Knowing I have to come up with a plan on how to unravel the lies I've spun, I decide to head out. Being around him clouds my head, and I need space to think.

Pulling open the door, I pause in the hallway. Not seeing Ryker, I move toward the front of the gym. As I come around the massive boxing ring, I spot him and Luke standing in front of a man in a suit. He's dressed like a businessman, but the rest of his appearance screams something more akin to sinister. I jerk to a halt when I hear their exchange.

"See, Ryker. That's where you're wrong. We don't forget. And we'll get what we want from you. Your family isn't impervious to us. Remember that."

"You motherfucker. You stay away from my family. They don't have anything to do with this, nor can they give you what you want. Get out before I call the cops."

It's obvious there is some history between them, and it's not good. I debate whether I should keep walking, but knowing what I need to do, I let my feet carry me forward until I'm standing between Ryker and Luke.

"Oh… um, Ryker." I step beside him, pressing my hand on his arm. My eyes glance between him and the mystery man briefly. "I'm going to head home for now. We can talk later… or tomorrow when I come in to work."

"I asked you to stay in my office, Addison."

He's obviously mad I didn't follow his instructions, but he doesn't control me. Gripping his chin in my fingers, I jerk his head so he's looking down at me.

"And I didn't listen to you. I have things I need to do, and waiting was taking forever." Pushing up on my toes, I brush my lips across Ryker's. "Call me later." She glances over at Luke. "Luke… see you tomorrow."

Hurrying away from the tense situation, I hurry over to my truck to leave. I rifle through my bag, trying to find my keys, when I finally give up and squat beside the driver's door and set it on the ground. Focused on removing the contents, I jump at the sound of someone talking.

"Find what you're looking for, Addison… I believe it was?"

Spinning too fast, I land on my ass. "Shit—you startled me." My eyes trail up and land on the man from inside. "Do you need something?"

He squats down beside me. "Not at the moment, but you looked like you needed some assistance." He picks up the scattered contents of my purse and places them back inside the bag. "A beautiful woman such as yourself should be taken care of."

Grunting at his sexist remark, I push to my feet.

"Look." I unlock my car and pull open the door. "I don't know who you are, but I don't need anyone to 'take'"—I make air quotes with my fingers—"care of me. If you'll excuse me, I need to be somewhere." I climb into the truck and toss my bag into the passenger seat.

"I apologize. I didn't mean to cause offense to you. But if you were my woman, you wouldn't be left so defenseless in a world where bad things could happen." His fingers wrap around the edge of my door. The massive gold signet ring on his finger flashes in the light as he leans in. "Take care, *Addison*. You never know where evil lurks."

The door closes, but my eyes are riveted to his tall frame as he walks away. His hands brush down the impeccable suit jacket as he straightens it while moving toward a dark SUV. Another man jumps out and opens the back door, but he stops and turns to face me. The look he gives sends chills down my spine, but I'm not one to show a man I'm intimidated, so I stare right back. The corner of his mouth twists into a foreboding smile as he climbs inside. His bodyguard, or whatever the other man is to him, closes the door and climbs back inside the front. Despite the nearly blackened windows, I have the distinct feeling his eyes are still on me.

Finally tearing my sights from his car, I crank up the engine and back out of my parking spot. Even after I pull out onto the road, I check the rearview mirror for the SUV. I don't know why, but I have a bad feeling about him. Forcing myself to forget about the fucked-up encounter, I pull into a Pack-N-Mail place. I need to set the wheels in motion for the truth to come out, and I think I have a pretty good idea how.

The bell over the door jingles as I step through the entrance and an older woman behind the counter smiles at me.

"Welcome. Anything I can help you with?" she calls out, watching me as I approach.

Setting my purse down, I drag out the folder. "Um… can you make a couple of copies for me? And then I'm going to need to mail something."

"Sure. It's twenty cents a page, and over there,"—she points to a rack against the wall—"you can grab the right size envelope, then I'll get you all set up."

Shuffling through the documents, I pull out the two I want to mail and hand them over.

"I need two copies of each of these, please. Then I'd like to mail them with a signature required, maybe certified?"

"All right. Give me a second to copy them. Grab an envelope and fill this out." She hands me a notepad. "Write who and where it needs to go to. I'll get it typed up and printed out."

She takes less than five minutes to make the copies and return to the counter. "Here are the original copies."

I stuff them back inside the manilla folder and stow it back inside my bag. Passing the paper with both names and address over to her, I tap my nails across the counter as I wait. My stomach is in knots with my decision to do this, but once she prints the label and places the sticky side down, there's no going back.

"That'll be seventeen-forty."

She hands me the receipt and tracking number, which I shove into the folder. Taking a deep breath, I leave the store feeling as though I just opened Pandora's box—and there's no closing it now. I rub my sweaty palms down on my leggings before climbing into my truck. It feels like someone's squeezing my chest in a death grip as the panic of what I've done filters through my system.

Before I realize it, I'm pulling into the parking garage of the hotel. As if on autopilot, I make it back to my room and slump against the closed door. I've done what I need to expose this fucked-up situation to Ryker, but now I have to face my boss, and I dread that as much as I do him realizing why I'm here.

My heart squeezes at the thought Ryker will think how I feel for him is an act to trick him—and maybe it started out that way, but now…

I palm my forehead and close my eyes. *Fuck*. Feelings for a man who doesn't have the capacity to commit, combined with my inability to hold on to a man is a recipe for disaster. But then again, the lies I've weaved will obliterate any chance of there being more. Forcing one foot in front of the other, I waltz over to the bed and drop to my ass on the edge. Pressing my face into my hands, I let my mind drift to the moment I boarded my heart up for good.

I push the button for the twelfth floor and take a breath to still my beating heart. My stomach knots with the uncertainty of what I'll find, but forcing myself to come here is necessary after David, my fiancé, canceled our dinner plans after being twenty minutes late.

After a gazillion phone calls and text messages, he finally responded with a simple message that said something had come up with a case... again. Being an attorney myself, I knew the hours could be long, depending on the case. Since David is a prosecutor for the state, I understand how consuming his job can be.

He and I met when I was a grad student finishing my law degree at the University of Georgia. David had also graduated from UGA and had been invited back as a guest lecturer. We hit it off immediately. David was fifteen years older than me, but he never seemed to let the age difference bother him. Now, twenty-five and working as a full-fledged lawyer, we decided the next step was marriage.

Lately, I feel as if he's pulling away. Stepping off the elevator, my gut tells me I'm not going to like what I find. Mostly, the floor of his office is dark, except for a few lights on in some of the smaller offices. David's office is toward the back, where I hope to find him. Walking as quietly as I can, I stop outside his closed door.

It doesn't take Sherlock Holmes to know what he's doing inside.

The moans and grunts are loud enough to be heard through the wooden barrier. Despite knowing my fiancé is inside with a woman who's not me, I have to see it for myself. Gripping the knob in my hand I inwardly groan that it's unlocked. Part of me hoped it wasn't.

Pushing the door open, I'm faced dead on with any woman's worse night-mare. There, with her legs held open by David, is the most beautiful woman. Her large breasts bounce as he rails into her. David's pants are down around his ankles, but his bare ass is out for God and everyone to see. Neither of them hears me open the door, which only means I get to watch as she cries out, and he grunts his release into her.

As her legs fall from his hands, he shifts, catching sight of me standing there with tears in my eyes.

"Addison." He speaks my name as he attempts to catch his breath.

My eyes drop to his now softened cock, the full condom clinging to his shaft.

"Why?" Is the only word I can muster when I finally meet his gaze.

"Seriously? You're asking me why?" He glances over his shoulder at the woman who sits up, grabbing at her discarded dress. "Look at her and look at you."

"What's that supposed to mean?" I ask, sucking in a painful breath. "I thought you loved me, David. We're getting married. You asked me to marry you."

"Things change."

"Guess so." Slipping the ring off my finger, I step forward and set it on the floor. "You could have been man enough to end it first, but I guess... you're not a man after all." Hot tears roll down my cheek as I turn to leave. I thought seeing him with his cock buried inside another woman was painful, but his next words shred me.

"Maybe if you looked more like her, you could've kept my attention. But you're nothing special. You're dumpy and not that great in bed, Addison. I'm a man who has needs. Looking and fucking like you do, you'll never keep a man, at least not a good-looking one. But hey... even fat people find love one day."

Lifting my chin, I turn to look over my shoulder.

"Fuck you, David."

Snapping out of the unwanted memory, I curl onto my side and close my eyes. David is right, though. I can't keep a man's attention, so there's no way I'll keep Ryker's. Not when he can have a woman just like the one who destroyed my life with David.

I just need this to be over—my heart is going to get hurt no matter what I do.

15

Ryker

"WHAT DO you mean he showed up at the gym?" Dallas leans forward in the booth. "Did you call the cops, Ry?"

"No. I don't want to deal with the cops unless I absolutely need to. I'm only telling you guys so you can be on the lookout for anything suspicious. He made some veiled threats, but that's just to try to force me into doing whatever it is they want from me." Sitting across from my siblings, I'm hit with emotion I struggle to contain.

My brothers and sister would do anything for me, and them being here proves it. I hate having to drag them back into my mess, but I don't trust Aleski Lipovsky or his fucking goons. Aleski is the head of the Russian Mafia in Phoenix. Unfortunately, his boxer is the one I accidentally killed. It wouldn't have happened if Ivan Gurin hadn't made side bets on our fight. But being greedy left him searching for ways to ensure he would win or the match got canceled. Rumors were that he was going to fight dirty during our match. Instead of canceling the event, I fought anyway. He got cocky and lost focus. One hit—and my life was changed forever.

"Do you think it's smart not to let the police know? He obviously wants something. He came all the way from Phoenix, or at least sent someone for him." Danika pops a peanut into her mouth as she watches me. "I mean… maybe they can beef up the patrol around your business."

"I'll be fine." Covering her hand with mine I smile. "It's you guys I'm worried about."

"Well,"—Griffyn taps the tabletop—"we can keep our eyes peeled. If he does something else, call the cops, though."

"Fine." I press the glass to my lips and take a sip.

"How's the hot receptionist working out?" Dallas smirks as he leans back in the seat. "Luke says she's got you all twisted up."

"Fucking Luke." Luke and Dallas are also friends, mainly because Luke frequents Dallas' club when he has the time. "Tell him to worry about being flogged and stay out of my business."

"So, it's true."

Glancing around at their faces, I know I'm not getting out of this conversation. While Dallas and Danika might believe in happily ever after, Griffyn and I don't. His reasons are different from mine, but neither of us want something permanent—or so I thought.

"She's different." I shrug my shoulder. "I don't know what that means, but I like her. You guys know me, I don't *do* commitment. And I've nearly fucked it up twice now, which means it's only a matter of time before I fuck up again."

Dallas snorts. "If you like her, then *don't* fuck it up. Besides, whatever you did must have not been that bad if she's giving you another shot."

"What's she look like? Big boobs, long legs, and let me guess… blonde?" Griffyn smirks as if he has my taste down to a science.

"Why are you all busting my balls? Jesus." I look down at the table, unwilling to see their reactions when I tell them about Addison. "For your information, she's five foot four-ish. No on the boobs, an ass you want to bite, and curves that have me wanting to get lost. And no,"—I palm the back of my neck—"she has dark brown hair." When I finally lift my gaze, Dallas and Griffyn are staring at me with a look of shock.

"Damn, brother. You've got it bad. I'm gonna have to come by the gym and see the chick that has you fucked up."

"Leave him alone." Danika rolls her eyes. "You idiots act like she's some kind of freak show. Maybe something different is exactly what this manwhore needs to settle down. Lord knows he's been through a ton of women."

"Hey, now." I elbow her. "I dated that one girl for almost a year, remember? The one I was with right when I made it big."

Danika stiffens in her seat. "I remember. She left you because she didn't want to deal with the fame."

"Probably for the best. I went kind of wild with the groupies." I chuckle at the memory of the endless stream of pussy when I first got signed. "But that's done and has been since getting out of prison." My gaze shifts to Griffyn. "Any more lawyers try to contact you again, Griff?"

"Nah, I haven't seen or heard from anyone, neither has Justin. Speaking of Justin, I may bring him with me when I swing by this week. He's interested in learning how to box."

"Great, bring him in. I'll have Luke show him around."

We fall into conversation about mundane stuff for the rest of our visit. Danika informs us she's taking a job as a mechanic for a local garage. It doesn't surprise us, seeing as she's a wiz with engines. We're just shocked it took her this long to do it. Danika has bounced around from job to job, never seeming to settle.

Dallas fills us in on our Uncle Dominick news. About six months ago, he met a woman in the club he owns and fell for her. He nearly lost her to some bookie she owed money to. It all happened so fast, he didn't bother telling Dallas until it had been settled. Now they're married. I never thought I'd see my uncle married. He was a lot like me and Griffyn, anti-relationship—or was. He called Dallas last night to tell him they were having a baby.

"I can't believe he's going to be a dad." Danika shakes her head. "Mom would've been so happy to be an aunt."

"Yeah." Griffyn mumbles. "I gotta run, guys." He stands, a noticeable change in his demeanor washed over him when Danika mentioned our mom. "I'll be by in the next day or two. Love you guys." He fist bumps each one of us, then heads out the door.

"Damn, talking about mom still puts him in a shitty mood. Don't get me wrong, I miss her and Byron, but it's been over a year since their death." Dallas gulps down his beer, the pain of losing our parents still etched in his eyes.

"We all grieve differently." Danika smiles. "I need to go as well. I'm meeting my new boss to sign some paperwork. I'll catch up with you guys later."

Dallas and I stay a little while longer, shooting the shit before going our separate ways. He has to get to the club before it opens, and I need to catch up on some paperwork at the gym. I put off opening this morning because I'm not sure what to say to Addison. She's going to ask me about Andrei, and I don't know what to tell her.

She needs to know he's dangerous, but telling her about him means giving her all of my dirty past—something I'm not really looking forward to.

Pulling into the parking lot my eyes immediately seek out her truck parked near the front of the building. I nestle my bike close to the building and fasten my helmet over the seat and head inside. Addison is at the desk, wearing a sleeveless blue satin top with a little black bow that ties around her neck. It hugs her body in a way that make her tiny tits look plump.

Moving to the side of the long counter, my gaze scans the rest of her. The shirt tucks into a flouncy black skirt that stops mid-thigh. Her short legs are elongated by the five-inch matching blue stiletto heels on her feet. My cock immediately presses against the zipper in my jeans. Beyond what she's wearing, it's the way her head is thrown back laughing at something one of our members is saying to her.

Jealousy courses through my veins, and I can't control myself. I step forward and wrap my arm around her waist. Jerking her body against mine, I grip her chin in a painful grip and claim her lips with my own. This kiss isn't soft—no, it's a message to the dick watching open-mouthed that Addison belongs to me. When I pull back from our heated greeting, I note her swollen lips and the heated gleam in her eyes. She stumbles slightly when I let go of her body and take a slight step back.

"Afternoon, Princess."

The fog clears from her vision, and she narrows her gaze on me.

"Ryker." Turning her head to the very shocked guy standing there, she plasters on a smile. "Sorry about that, Michael. I should get to work. Thanks for the chat, though. Enjoy the rest of your day."

"Um… sure. You, too. Ryker." He nods at me as he hurries into the gym.

"What in the *fuck* was that?" She folds her arms across her chest. "You can't do that shit, Ryker. It's not professional."

"I don't give a fuck about professionalism, Addison. What I do care about is another man encroaching on what's mine."

"Yours? I don't belong to you." She huffs throwing her arms into the air. "And even if I did, he wasn't flirting. We were just talking."

"You're blind, sweetheart. That man… hell, any man takes one look at you and their dicks immediately stand at attention. He wasn't talking, he was flirting."

"You're stupid. Look at me, Ryker. He wasn't flirting, I assure you."

"Look at you? Fuck, Addison. You have no clue how fucking gorgeous you are, do you?" I step forward, pressing her back into the counter. My cock is already dangerously close to ripping out of my pants, and having her pressed against me isn't helping. "Feel what you do to me? I promise you, he isn't that far off from having the same problem."

"Ryker, this is nuts." She presses her palms against my chest. "You and I make little sense together. You can have any woman you want… someone who doesn't look like me."

I start to retort, but the clearing of a voice behind her has me looking away.

"What?" I snap at the interruption standing at the counter holding something.

"I'm looking for Ryker Nash."

Addison stiffens beneath me as I lean forward.

"I'm Ryker Nash."

"I need you to sign for this, please." He hands over an envelope and holds out a tablet. I scribble my name across the screen and take the large envelope from his grasp. "Have a good day."

Pulling the heavy paper toward me, I glance down and furrow my brows. It's not labeled like the other certified shit I get from law offices trying to get my business with their ambulance-chasing promises of winning big—all of which land right in the trash without even opening.

"What the fuck is this?"

Addison steps out from between me and the counter and shrugs.

"I'll be back. I need to use the ladies' room while you figure out"— she arches her brow as she flicks her gaze down at the manilla paper weight clutched in my fingers—"what that is."

16

Addison

Fuck.

I knew the damn thing would be delivered while I was here, but I hadn't really thought about how it would make me feel. Was I being a coward for not just telling him myself? *Probably*. Didn't change a damn thing, though. The letter was now in his hands, and his life would be irrevocably changed.

Thinking about what was going through his mind made me wonder if the same letter had already been delivered in Atlanta. I'm not sure why my boss hadn't sent the information to the other party involved before this, seeing as they were deeply entwined in the mess, too. I had been shocked to find that tidbit of information buried in the stack of papers I'd been finally given access to before coming to Nashville.

Splashing water on my face, I take several deep breaths and plaster on a fake smile before stepping out of the bathroom. Part of me wants to hide out in the bathroom forever, but I'm pretty sure it will make me look guilty of something—and I don't need him asking me a ton of questions.

As soon as I emerge from the bathroom, Luke is leaning against the wall outside his door.

"I wouldn't go in there right now. He's kinda of having a freak out."

He didn't need to tell me because the sounds coming from inside Ryker's office are almost animalistic. Something loud crashes against the door and I jerk.

"What happened?"

"Dunno. Whatever was inside that envelope set him off like a fourth of July fireworks extravaganza. Only it's not pretty."

Blowing out a deep breath I step around Luke and fist the doorknob.

"I'm going in. He needs someone to calm him down, or he'll destroy the entire fucking place."

Pushing open the door, I can't stifle my gasp. The office looks like a bomb has gone off and decimated everything in its path. Whatever was on the surface of the desk is now scattered across the floor, some of it in shreds. His laptop is in fractured shards beneath the wall where it was obviously thrown. Easing through the opening, I push the door closed behind me and scan the inside. Ryker is on the floor beside the bathroom with his head buried in his hands. The cushions on the couch are ripped to pieces and the cotton filling floats around the office like winter in New York. The only thing not destroyed is the mail at his feet. And by mail, I mean the letter I sent him. The one he doesn't know I'm involved with.

"Ryker." The whisper of his name squeaks out into the silence. "What happened?" My stomach churns with bile seeing as I know exactly what led him to this outburst.

"Everything." He sounds so broken as he mutters without looking up. "My entire life is a fucking lie."

"What can I do? How can I help?" My heart breaks for this man whose world has been upended.

He pushes to his feet suddenly, making me step back on instinct.

"Help me? You can't do a fucking thing, Addison." He comes toward me like a rabid animal, ready to attack.

"Ryker, calm down." I press my hand into his chest as he steps closer. "Seriously. You're scaring me."

"You want to help me, Addison?" His hand reaches out, gripping the tie to my shirt. "Your perfect little existence and life can't do shit for me except mask the pain."

Before I can respond, he rips the black bow holding my silk shirt closed, tearing my top down the front.

"Don't do this, Ryker… you're too angry right now."

Ignoring my plea, his free hand reaches beneath my skirt and shreds the lace thong I'm wearing. His fingers slip up my chest and wrap around my throat, causing me to grab at his hands.

"I'm taking what I want, Addison. And based on this,"—he roughly shoves his other fingers into my channel—"you want it, too."

My body might respond to this man's touch, but my brain is screaming at me that this is all wrong. He's filled with a rage that terrifies me, but his grip on my neck is just tight enough to keep my words silenced. He backs me against the wall and with one arm, lifts my feet from the floor. My legs wrap around him out of fear of strangulation, but he takes it as acquiescence. The tips of my nails dig into the flesh of his forearms, embedding themselves into his skin. One of my heels clatters to the floor behind him.

Ryker bites and nips at my neck—not gently—before covering my mouth with his own. All the while, he frees his cock and roughly shoves himself inside me. Despite being soaked for him, it doesn't feel like the other times we've had sex—this is punishment. I whimper at the intrusion, giving him the chance to press his tongue between my lips. His thrusts are unforgiving as he takes what he wants, and all I can do is hold on with my eyes pinched shut. This isn't tender by any stretch of the imagination, and I can't stop the tears from welling in my eyes.

Ryker peels his lips from mine and presses his face to my lace covered breast. The pain is intense as he bites down through the material making my eyes pop open. He's in his own world as I watch as the cords of his neck tighten and his head tilts to the ceiling. His body continues to pound into mine as he tightens his grip further around my neck, his fingers threatening to cut off my air. It doesn't take long before I feel the heat of his cum jetting inside me, and he roars out his release.

Ryker loosens his hold on my neck, and I desperately gasp for air, filling my lungs with oxygen. My legs drop to the floor, and I slide down the wall, unable to hold myself up. Scrambling to my knees, I crawl around his legs and grab my toppled heel. Tugging the remaining one off I stand and clutch them against my chest, frantically trying to close my blouse. Ryker casts a vacant glance at me, his eyes devoid of any emotion.

What the fuck just happened?

Holding the flimsy pieces of fabric closed, I unlock his office door and escape. I don't miss the wide-eyed expressions of several of the members as I fumble behind the desk for my purse, still trying to keep my clothes together, nor do I miss Luke as he snaps out of his shocked stupor and calls out to me.

"Addison... wait."

Ignoring him, I practically fall out the front entrance when I push through the doors. Recovering my balance, I lose my grip on my shoes and bag as they tumble to the cement. Dropping to my knees, I scramble to scoop the spilled contents up, but the tears have broken through the dam, and I can't see through the waterfall of emotions pouring out.

"Fuck." Arms wrap around my body. "I got you, Addison." Luke scoops me off the ground, grabbing my things, and starts toward the entrance.

"No. Please... I just want to go home." I sob against him as I try to wiggle free of his hold. "I can't go back in there."

Pausing, Luke seems to have some kind of internal debate with himself before finally turning back to the parking lot.

"Fine, but I'm taking you there. You're in no condition to drive."

Carrying me over to my truck, he shifts his hold on me to dig out the keys from my bag and opens the door. Setting me inside, he reaches across the seat and buckles me in. Luke stares at me for a moment, like he wants to ask me a question, but refrains. I watch as he shuts the door and hurries around to climb in beside me.

Drawing my feet onto the seat, I wrap my arms around my knees and sob. Luke's soft touch startles me out of my breakdown, causing me to look at him.

"Addison, did... did Ryker, um..." He stumbles on his words, but I already know what he going to ask me. Hell, the way I look, I don't blame him. "Did Ryker assault you?"

"No, Luke. Things just got carried away… that's all." I glance away from him briefly. "You warned me not to go in there. I deserved what I got."

"Are you fucking kidding me? Addison…" He grips the steering wheel to the point of making his knuckles turn white. "You say he didn't rape you, and I want to believe my best friend isn't capable of that, but looking at you right now… I gotta be honest, Doll. I'm not real confident you're telling me the truth."

"I didn't tell him no or stop." *Granted, I couldn't speak, but Luke doesn't need to know that.*

"Doesn't matter. If you didn't say yes to this, it might as well be the same thing." Luke grumbles something under his breath. "I don't give a fuck if he found out earth shattering news.. you don't treat someone you care about like a fuck toy."

Luke pulls into the hotel parking garage and parks. He watches as I fight with my shirt, trying to make myself look presentable for the elevator ride to my room.

"*Fuck.*" He mutters as he reaches behind his head and strips off his shirt. "Here, put this on, Addi. Do you need me to walk you up?"

My chest constricts at the tenderness in his voice and from hearing him call me by my nickname. Luke and I haven't been exactly friendly with each other, so seeing the worry etched on his face is something I don't expect.

"No. Thank you Luke." Taking the fabric from his hands, I pull it over my head. "How are you going to get back?" I question, realization setting in that he drove my truck.

"I'll call for a ride. Don't worry about me."

I nod my head at him. "Thank you, for this. Luke, I won't be back at work. I'm going back to Atlanta tonight. Can you please tell Ryker for me?"

"I'm sorry, Addison." Luke's expression morphs into one of shame and sadness. "I should have stopped you from going in there. I know how he can get, but this is new… even for him."

"It's not your fault. Thanks for this," I finger the t-shirt. "I'll mail it back to you."

"No… keep it, Addi." He reaches across the console and pulls me into a hug before climbing out of the truck. "Take care of yourself."

Getting out of the truck, I sling my bag over my shoulder, grip the door in my hand and look over at Luke, who is walking toward the front entrance.

"Can you do me a favor? No matter what happens next, know that I was falling in love with your friend. But sometimes things aren't meant to be, and people aren't who we think they are. Be safe, Luke."

Slamming the door, I hurry across the pavement without giving him a second glance. I knew what I was doing had risks. Knew things might blow up in my face. What I didn't expect is how badly I hurt now that it's happened. Not only did he humiliate me—he shattered my heart to smithereens. And the worst part? He has no idea.

Time to go back to Atlanta and put this mess behind me.

17

Ryker

I KEEP my hands against the hard surface as I struggle to breathe. *What the fuck is wrong with me?* I vaguely hear the door open, signaling Addison's rapid departure, but that doesn't motivate me to move or tell her to stay. Everything I ever believed about my childhood is a lie.

Shoving off the wall, I turn in a slow circle in my office. I really destroyed the place. Papers are shredded and scattered across the floor. My couch, rather what's left of it, is spilling the insides onto the floor like molten lava. Several holes decorate the once pristine paint where my fists went through the sheetrock in my fit of rage. Glancing at the ground, I spot the offending letter that started this whole fucked-up rage of destruction. Bending down, I snatch it off the floor and move to my desk. It's miraculously the only item in the room not damaged from my little outburst.

Little. I snort at my thought. There wasn't anything little about what I did. Righting the toppled desk chair, I plop down and finger the parchment. While the outside of the envelope isn't very telling, what's on the inside is like opening Pandora's box.

My eyes glance over at the words that will alter the course of my life moving forward.

> *Abernathy & Fitzgerald*
> *Family Law*
> *12074 3rd Street*
> *Atlanta, Georgia 30047*
> *RE: Dominic/Winston*
>
> *To Whom it May Concern,*
> *Please find attached a letter left by Mr. Cyrus Dominic regarding some unfinished matters regarding the estate of Calvin Winston. Once you've read the letter, please contact us to determine how to move forward.*
> *Sincerely,*
> *J. Abernathy*
> *Attorney at Law*

When I first read the note, I thought it was a mistake—I didn't know how Calvin Winston, the billionaire murdered by his own son after killing his wife, fit together with my grandfather. And frankly, I don't think I cared.

Then curiosity gets the better of me, and I turn the page again.

My eyes become laser-focused on the document, and I cringe. Our grandfather was not a nice man. When he died, I felt nothing but relief. Pretty sure my siblings did as well. He was a dick our whole life growing up but became even more unbearable after my mother died. It was like anything that might have been good inside him withered up and disappeared the day we lowered her and my stepdad into the ground.

Taking a deep breath, I let myself read over the words one more time—words that aren't even meant for me.

Dear Griffyn,

If you're reading this, it means I have left this world to meet my maker and reunite with my daughter and granddaughter. There are so many things I should say to you, but nothing will make what I have to say better.

I was not a good man—but you already know this. When I was young, I made some terrible choices that inevitably altered the course of my life. For so long, I grew up knowing I was going to fight for the underdog... rising from a lowly attorney into the man on the bench. But becoming a Superior Court Judge only left me vulnerable to the evils that plague this world.

You see, I fell prey to the glitz and glamor gambling could provide. That lifestyle led me to a man I would never rid myself of again. The who is not important, it's the 'what' that followed that changed things. Becoming indentured to this person left me with sins I'll never be able to atone for. Mistakes I cannot take back.

The biggest mistake was your father.

He was the evilest of them all, but he was in bed with the same monster I was, only he was loyal to them in a way I could never be. That made him untouchable. When he began courting your mother, I pleaded for him to stop. When she fell pregnant with you, I insisted he marry her and make the union appear legit. He and I both had too much to lose if their relationship blew up. Your mother was a force to be reckoned with, and I knew she would expose everything we worked hard to keep hidden from the light.

The day you were born, nothing could have prepared me for the events that followed. Lives were altered, families destroyed, and lies fortified in stone. For a while, things seemed to hold together. No one was the wiser about what was truly going on—but I was wrong... so wrong.

You were seventeen when your mother got the phone call that would begin to unravel the tangled web I'd been part of creating. To you and your brothers, Seth Winters is your father—but his name was not Seth. In order to keep up the ruse, we forged documents to ensure no one would ever find out he was not who he claimed. And it worked... until his death.

Your mother learned of the treachery shortly after meeting Byron. But much like the money had bought silence in the past, I kept the truth hidden again. Days before I was to take my final breath, information was brought to light. Information that left me with a rage I never knew I possessed. And in that final moment, I knew I needed to tell you the truth, no matter how hard it would be for you to hear.

I hope you can forgive me or at minimum, find peace in knowing this had nothing to do with you and everything to do with the decision I made as a young, stupid boy. While there is so much more to tell you, I cannot fathom spilling any more secrets. Those will come out in due time.

Griffyn, I'm so sorry for the hurt I weaved around you and your brothers.

Seth Winters was your father. That much is true. Did you ever wonder why it was so easy for Byron to adopt you boys after he and Meghan married? Well, my boy, that's because Seth Winters does not exist—not on paper. Knowing I've left you with nothing but my troubles, you deserve to get what's entitled to you.

Seth Winters was, in fact, Calvin Winston.

Sincerely,

Cyrus Dominic

Slamming the paper down onto the surface of my desk, I bend down and fumble around on the floor until I find my cell phone. I knocked it off in my temper tantrum earlier. Dragging my finger across the screen, I hesitate. Griffyn will lose his shit faster and probably more violently than me, but the damn letter was addressed to him. Shaking away my nerves, I press on the contact picture for my sister. She's usually the voice of reason, even if she's batshit crazy any other time.

"Ryker, what's up?" Her voice is barely a whisper.

Glancing at the screen, I shake off the confusion, seeing as it's a little after one, "Did I wake you?"

"Um… no… I was just," I can hear her shuffling in the background, and a low rumble of voices is muffled through the phone. "Sorry. I'm not at home. You okay? You sound funny."

"No, I'm not. Can you come to the gym?"

Her silence speaks volumes. I've never admitted to needing anything, so hearing me say I wasn't okay is probably freaking her out.

"Yeah. Give me about ten minutes, and I'll head over. Anyone else coming?"

"Not yet. I haven't called anyone else, and I won't until you get here and help me figure out some shit."

"Are you in trouble, Ry?"

"No…" I shake my head, despite the fact she can't see me. "But it's bad, Danika, and I don't know what to do." Luke steps through my door wearing only a pair of shorts, making me arch a brow in question. "Look, just get here as soon as you can. I've got to go."

"Okay. Love you, Ry."

"Love you too, Dani."

Tossing my phone onto the wooden top, I lean back and sigh. I'm completely caught off guard by Luke's words as he steps into my office.

"What in the fuck did you do to her?"

Confusion muddles my expression, and I glance around the room. "To who?"

"Addison, you fuckwit. I just took her home, Ryker. She was a sobbing mess. And don't let me get started on how she looked beyond that. Did you fucking rape her?"

"What?" I push up from my chair, the plastic frame clattering into the wall. "Why in the fuck would you ask me something like that?"

"Oh… I don't know. Maybe because she ran out of your office with her shirt ripped open. She barely got out the front door before collapsing. So you tell me, Ryker… what the fuck happened?"

My eyes drop to the floor beside him, and I blink, uncertain I'm seeing what I think. Luke follows my line of sight and bends down to pick it up.

"Wow. I don't even know what to say about this." Shaking his head, he tosses the shredded remnants of her cobalt panties at me.

Snatching it out of the air, I clasp it in a fist. Shoving my empty hand into my hair, I tug on the strands and scream, *"Fuck."*

"You got that right, man. I don't know what the fuck is going on, but that… what I saw in her eyes and how she looked is something I never want to see again."

His words hit me like a fucking jab to the jaw, and I stumble backward into my chair. Snippets of what we—no, I did—earlier parade across my vision like a movie on replay.

"I was out of my head, Luke. I shouldn't have touched her, but I was so fucked up with rage I wasn't in my right mind. Did I hurt her?"

"She said she wasn't, but man, I don't believe her. She looked so fucking destroyed. What got you so fucked up that you hurt the woman you were falling for, Ry?"

"This." I hand him the stack of papers and watch as he glances over them.

"Holy shit."

"Yeah…" I shake my head in disgust. "And now not only has my life imploded, I lost the only girl I think I might be in love with. Where is she? The hotel?"

"Man, I hate to tell you this, but she was heading back to Atlanta tonight. Said to tell you she quit. But Ryker, she said something that tells me you may have a chance to fix this fucked-up situation."

"What do you mean?" I take the papers back from him and shove them into the folder on my desk.

Luke palms the back of his head. "When she got out of the truck… by the way, you owe me because I had to catch an Uber shirtless since you destroyed her top. Anyway… she said, 'Can you do me a favor? No matter what happens next, know that I fell in love with your friend. But sometimes things aren't meant to be, and people aren't who we think they are.'"

"I need to go after her. To make this right… what I did…" My words are cut off when Danika waltzes into the office.

"What in the fuck happened in here?" Her eyes widen as she looks around my trashed office.

All thoughts of going after Addison come to a screeching halt as I shove the folder at my sister. I watch in apt fascination as her face goes through a series of emotions. First sadness, then rage, and finally shock. She slams the folder closed.

"Is this for real?" She holds it out, shaking it in front of me. "Are you telling me that your father is actually Calvin Winston? How do you know this isn't some sort of fucked-up ruse to get you into their office?"

Shrugging his shoulders, Luke interjects, "It says their firm deals in family law. They wouldn't be looking to sue the state like an ambulance chaser would."

"So? Doesn't make it any truer. Where's your computer?" She scans the space, her eyes landing on the cracked device. "Really? You fucking moron, you destroyed that, too?"

"I'll grab mine." Luke hurries out of the room to fetch his laptop from his office.

"What the hell am I going to do, Danika?"

"First, we're going to see if this firm is legit. Then you're going to call them, and if they can confirm this is real, we'll call Dallas and Griffyn." She paces the floor as she talks. "What other secrets are there?"

"What do you mean?" I furrow my brows in confusion.

"It says, *I cannot fathom spilling any more secrets. Those will come out in due time.* That clearly means there's more, Ryker. And seedy people? What the hell was Grandfather involved in?"

"Here." Luke steps in, thrusting the machine at me. "Pull up Google."

Once the machine is powered up and I have Google opened, I type in the attorney's name. Immediately, the firm pops up on the screen, and I glance at him and Danika. Taking a deep breath, I click the link and watch as the home page of a distinguished-looking logo appears. Navigating around, I read that they, in fact, deal with family law. A strange tingle at the back of my neck has me hovering over to *meet the staff*. With one click, my world crumbles even more. Nothing—not this letter or the revelation my father wasn't who I believe him to have been—strikes me as painfully as what I'm staring at right now.

"Fuck." Luke grumbles beside me, shaking his head.

"What?" Danika moves beside him and stares down at the screen. "Who's that?"

"That, my dear sister,"—swallowing down the bile burning inside my throat, I spin around the laptop so the screen is facing her better—"is one more person I love who's nothing but a liar."

Staring at us from the sixteen-inch screen is Addison Quincy, *Attorney* at Law.

18

Addison

THE LOUD POUNDING on my door lulls me from my fitful sleep. I got home after six and emptied what was left in my bottle of wine. Now, the sound of someone hammering has my head throbbing even more. Peeling myself off the couch, I stumble my way to the entry of my apartment and look through the peephole, only to find my best friend, Libby, staring at the glass hole I'm watching her through.

"I know you're in there, Addi. Open this fucking door right now."

Sighing, I unlock the deadbolt and tug open the door. "Please, Libby. I'm not in the mood."

Her eyes trail my haggard appearance. "Well, looking like that, I don't care if you're in the mood. What the fuck happened in Nashville? And why in the hell are you wearing that?"

Fingering Luke's t-shirt, I shrug. "I was in a hurry to leave and didn't change. Then I got home and well,"—I wave toward the now empty bottle of wine—"I might have drank myself to sleep."

"And why are you wearing a t-shirt over your silk blouse, Addi?" Libby folds her arms across her chest and taps her heel on the carpeted floor. "Did something happen that you're not telling me? When you called me and said everything blew up and you were headed home, I knew something else happened by the tone in your voice. I mean, hell, you were completely into Ryker. So speak… don't leave a damn thing out."

Shaking my head at her, I force the bile down in my throat. The signs of my drinking are churning in my gut, and my head is swimming with dizziness.

"I know you mean well, Lib, but right now, I'm slightly drunk and desperate to take a shower and sleep. Plus, I need some time to think about everything that's happened. And then… and only then, will I be in the mindset to tell you."

"Promise?" She tilts her head at me in question, worry marring her beautiful features.

"Promise."

"Fine." Libby wraps her arms around me and squeezes. "I'll give you until tomorrow. I'll be here at nine, and we'll go to breakfast."

"Don't you work?"

"I'm taking the morning off. I was in court when you called earlier, and that case is all wrapped up. I'll call Mr. Abernathy in the morning to let him know I'll be in a little late. You aren't getting out of talking, Addi."

"Fine." I walk to the door and grip the knob. "I'll be ready tomorrow."

Giving her one last hug, I bolt the door and press my head against the cool surface. *How did my life become this fucked up?* Walking into my bedroom, I glance over at the suitcase still leaning against the wall. I can't bring myself to empty it right now because it will signify the ending mess I left in Nashville. Inside the bathroom, I stare at my reflection in the mirror. Looking back at me is a woman I don't recognize.

Her eyes are swollen from the gallons of tears cried today. My normally pulled-together chocolate hair is a ragged mess, closely resembling someone who hasn't showered or brushed it in days. But that's not why it looks like someone ruffled my head—no, that style directly results from Ryker's rough display of ownership of my body. My hair, looking like it does, is a visual reminder of the rough way he took me against the wall.

The red marks that marred my neck have since faded, but even as I reach up and finger the imaginary spot where they were, I can still feel his hands on me. Closing my eyes, I brace my hands on the vanity and take several deep breaths. Gathering my strength, I strip off the t-shirt Luke so graciously gave me and toss it onto the floor. The once pristine satin shirt lays across my skin in a tattered mess. The black bow on the collar hangs by a thread against the shredded material. Peeling it over my shoulders, I let it drop to the floor beside the cotton tee. I reach behind my back and peel off my bra— the bra that somehow managed to stay on. Though it didn't deter Ryker from marking me with his teeth. Perfectly shaped teeth marks litter the tops of my boobs. Turning away from the painful reminder, I straighten my spine and step to the glass enclosure to flick on the faucet.

As the water heats and steam begins to fill the stall, I shove the black skirt down my hips and step out of it. Kicking it to the side, I grab the railing and step into the shower. The hot water pelts my skin as I move beneath the spray. Bracing my hands against the wall, I drop my head to my chest and try to slow my breathing. No matter how hard I try, the tears begin to beat against my eyelids. Sobs wrack my body as the emotions I was certain I was done with pour out of me like river rapids.

When the water finally runs cold, I turn the handle off and climb out. The soft padded mat beneath my feet does little to ease the pain I'm riddled with. Wrapping a fluffy white towel around my body, I walk dripping wet into my bedroom. Uncaring of the consequences to my bed, I climb beneath the sheets and curl into a ball. I should hate Ryker for what he did, but no matter how I try to convince myself, that's not the emotion I conjure. Instead, deep-seated heartbreak is all I feel. Somehow, amid the lies, I fell in love with him—then ripped his world apart.

I deserve the pain.

I don't remember falling asleep, but once more I'm startled awake by the rapid fire knocking coming from the living room. Pushing to my feet, I drop the towel and sift through my dresser for a tank top and shorts. Once I pull them on, I hurry into the hallway and head straight for the door.

Yanking it open, I'm greeted with a furious scowl.

"Why aren't you dressed?" Libby pushes past me, grumbling her displeasure.

"I just woke up." Slamming the door I turn to my friend. "Give me a few minutes, and I'll be ready."

Running to my room, I quickly pull off the shorts and shirt I just put on and grab some underwear and a bra. Slipping them on, I snag a maxi dress from my closet and tug it over my head. Shoving my feet into flip-flops, I rush into the bathroom. With little care about how I look, I pull my locks into a ponytail and brush my teeth.

"Okay," I greet Libby in the kitchen. "I'm ready. Sorry… I forgot to set an alarm, and my phone is dead."

"You didn't charge it?" She shakes her head. "Here, give it to me. We'll plug it in while we're gone." She connects it to a charger she found in a kitchen drawer and turns to face me. "Let's go."

Following my beautiful friend out the door, I can't help but smile. Libby is a force to be reckoned with. With her fiery red hair and killer long legs, she makes most men stop dead on the street. Not to mention her sarcastic wit and intelligence leaves most wondering what the hell just happened when she breezes past them. When she finds a man who can handle her passion… God help *him*.

I climb into her BMW and buckle up as she ambles around to the driver's side. Her car matches her personality to a tee with its candy red exterior.

"Where are we going?"

"Busy Bee Café."

The ride is mostly silent. I'm sure Libby knows I'm not ready to talk. Which I'm thankful for because I don't know what to tell her. How do I explain that I fell in love with a man incapable of feelings? A man who destroyed me emotionally and physically. And despite that, I still love him.

God, I'm fucked up.

"Addi, we're here." She pulls the keys from the ignition and slides out of the car.

I didn't realize we had stopped. Jesus, I'm out of it. Climbing from the safety of her car, I follow her inside. The place is busy, but somehow, she snags us a table near the windows. Sliding into the plastic chair, I pick up the menu and pretend to read the contents.

The truth is, I'm not hungry, but Libby is like a dog with a bone and will bite my head off if I don't eat something. The waitress pops by, takes our orders, then whisks off to the back.

"Alright. Times up, Addi. Start talking."

Blowing out a breath, I pinch the bridge of my nose. "I don't even know where to start."

"Doesn't matter where you begin. It's where you end."

I look at my friend as if she's a grown a horn. Her words hold so much more power than I think she realizes. Glancing to the side, I can't help but notice a man sitting across from a girl who could be Libby's twin. She's speaking to her companion, and I can't seem to look away. His sole focus is on her, and all I can see is the look of pure adoration. It's obvious he loves her deeply. He must sense me staring because his gaze shifts to me, and I suck in a breath. His deep eyes narrow as he looks at me, searching for recognition. His wife or girlfriend, or whoever she is to him, places her hand on his arm, jerking him back to their conversation. There is a weird sense of familiarity with him, but I brush it off and turn back to Libby.

"I should have never lied about who I was."

Libby shakes her head. "It's too late to think about that, Addi."

"I know, but still... I didn't mean for things to start between Ryker and me, but they did. God, when we come together, it's like a detonation I've never experienced. At first it was sex, at least that's what I tell myself. And the longer I let the lie go on, the harder it was to tell him. That's why I did what I did. I thought maybe I could let him know what brought me to Nashville without actually telling him I was involved. Only everything blew up anyway."

"What do you mean? You still haven't told me what made you leave abruptly."

"I mailed letters with the information to both Ryker and Drake Winston. I figured it was time to bring both families into the fold. Only I didn't really prepare myself for Ryker's reaction when he got the certified envelope." I take a sip of my water before continuing. Just thinking about his behavior makes my throat tighten with regret. "He went ballistic, Libby. Locked himself in his office and tore it into shambles. I should have listened to Luke."

"Luke? The best friend?"

"Yeah. He told me to leave him alone, that going into his office was a bad idea. But I thought, in my infinite stupidity, I could calm him down."

"I'm assuming you didn't?"

"No. He wanted to take control of his life, and since he couldn't, I became the thing he could control. I won't go into details, but Luke took me home when I finally left his office."

"And gave you a shirt. Because you couldn't wear yours, could you?"

"No. I can still feel him, Libby. The way he was with me was frightening, but he was so broken. And I caused that—*me*. No one else. When he learns the truth, he'll hate me even more."

"His anger doesn't give him the right to hurt you, Addi. And based on what I'm hearing you say without saying it, he did that right? He hurt you more than emotionally?"

Biting down on my lip to quell the tears forming, I simply nod. "I deserved it."

"Jesus Christ, Addi. No one deserves to be hurt physically. You should press charges."

"Absolutely not." I jerk my gaze to her. "He wasn't in his right mind, Libby. He was hurting, and if allowing him that moment to assuage his pain, even if it was just a fraction, I'd do it again."

"We'll have to agree to disagree with this." She stops talking when the waitress appears with our food. "So what now?"

I watch as our server scurry away.

"Now, I wait." I sigh. "He'll probably call the office, and I'll have to face the betrayal when it happens."

Libby tilts her head, watching me closely. "Wow… you really did fall for him, didn't you?"

"Yeah, but it doesn't matter. I lied to him, making me no different from the monster he called a father."

After we finish breakfast, I promise to see Libby at work tomorrow and climb from the car. Everything about this morning makes me feel even worse than I did last night. Saying the truth out loud to Libby and admitting I was in love with someone who would never be mine hurts like a motherfucker. Part of me wants to quit my job and move far away to start over, but I've worked so hard to get where I am. Lost in thought, I don't notice someone waiting by my door.

I glance around the hallway at the neighboring apartments, wondering if he's at the wrong one. There's a small niggling of something in the back of my head about this guy, but I shove it aside as I get closer to him. He's dressed in a fancy suit and definitely out of place standing there.

"Can I help you with something?"

"Actually." He steps forward and smiles. "You sure can."

19

Ryker

"YOU SURE YOU want to do this?" Dallas presses his palm against my shoulder, nodding toward the entrance of the law firm. "It's not too late to let me and Griffyn handle things."

The building Abernathy & Fitzgerald occupies is in downtown Atlanta, nestled between several other large ones. The street is lined with cars and people as they make their way to their end destinations. Much like Nashville, it's noisy and filled with people clueless about the evils of the world around them. For a moment, I let myself wonder what it was like for Calvin Winston when he was alive. *Does his family live near here?* Shoving those thoughts aside, I glance over at my brother.

"I need to do this. She lied to me about who she was, but we left things..." My voice trails off, remembering our last moments together. "This is going to suck on several levels, Dallas, but like a ruined Band-Aid, I need to rip it off to heal."

"Christ, you fell for her." Griffyn jerks open the door. "Not that you're going to listen to me, but perhaps this and her feelings for you are separate. Did you consider that?"

Stepping into the massive lobby, we navigate toward the elevators off to the side. I don't miss the gaping stares as we walk crowded together like some kind of mob. Hell, my brothers are good-looking guys, too, we share the same genetics after all, so it's not surprising we attract attention wherever we go. Dallas presses the button for fourteen. Apparently, the office has the entire floor to themselves. As the elevator ascends, Griffyn's words bounce around in my head like a pinball machine. I want to believe her feelings were real, but her whole existence in Nashville was a farce.

"Luke warned me to check into her, and I was going to, but things happened, and I forgot. By that time, she'd been there too long to care. If I had…"

"You would have known she was an attorney. But Ryker," Dallas pauses, his eyes searching me for something. "She's not trying to get money out of you. Not like the others. Maybe she was scared to tell you the truth after getting to know you."

"Maybe." That's all I say as the doors open and we step into the lobby.

Immediately, I know we're not dealing with a dime-store law office. This place exudes class with the marble floor and glass chandelier hanging over the reception desk. Scanning the area, my eyes land on an older woman walking toward the counter. Seeing the three of us standing there, she stumbles slightly before composing herself.

"Hello. Can I help you?" She straightens her spine as she sets down the file in her hand.

Griffyn steps forward and quickly turns on the charm with his killer smile.

"Yes, ma'am. We have an appointment with Miss Quincy."

"Oh…" Her eyes widen a fraction. "I'm sorry, Miss Quincy didn't come in today. Let me grab Mr. Abernathy for you. If you wouldn't mind having a seat, I'll be right back."

Furrowing my brows, I glance over at Dallas. "She didn't show up to work?"

"Gentlemen." A deep voice cuts off my thoughts, drawing all of our attention to the hallway where the receptionist disappeared seconds ago. "I'm sorry for the inconvenience. When you called yesterday, the plan was for Miss Quincy to be back at work, but unfortunately, she didn't come in today. I'll be meeting with you instead." He sticks his hand out to Griffyn, who's standing the closest. After shaking hands with my brother, he motions for us to follow him. "Mr. Nash, if you and your brothers would follow me, please."

We follow him down the sterile hallway into a massive conference room. In the center of the space is a large glass table with multiple chairs around it. Taking a cue from him, we pile inside and sit down.

"I don't mean to be blunt, but your case has been quite tricky for us."

Griffyn gapes at the older man. "What do you mean?"

"Certified mail, phone calls, emails… have all gone unreturned by you three. I'd all but filed this in my drawer until some other cases cleared up and I could devote the time to the sensitive matter." He leans back in his chair. "But Miss Quincy was determined to find you to prove she was partner material. That and she felt this was a matter that deserved the utmost focus." He laughs as he flips open the folder. "Of course she didn't know all the details before volunteering to go to Nashville in person. I felt bad after she left, knowing the shitstorm this case was going to generate."

"Wait… you're telling me she had no idea of the details?" I speak, leaning my arms on the table as I stare at him. "She blindly walked into a family mess all because she thought we needed to know about the will?"

"That's precisely what I'm saying, Mr. Nash. Miss Quincy is a damn fine attorney in court, but outside of the legal system, she doesn't have a malicious bone in her body. I've often wondered why a woman like her is in family law."

"A woman like her?" My eyes cut to Griffyn, who until he spoke, I thought was simply taking this all in. "What does that mean?"

"Miss Quincy is a romantic at heart and one of the kindest women I've come to know. I'm not sure how she got you here, but I assure you it was done with your family's best interest at heart. That's just how she operates. Now…" He slides a slip of paper over toward me. "We can't complete this until the other party can meet with us, but I'd like to go over the details with you in private first."

Dallas finally breaks the silence. "I don't understand. What other party needs to be present?"

Mr. Abernathy takes off his glasses and sighs. He scans each one of our faces. A look of sympathy washes over his eyes as he sits straighter in his chair.

"Mr. Nash… Dallas, may I call you that?" Dallas shakes his head yes, waiting for him to continue. "You're entitled to a part of Calvin Winston's fortune. Do you understand what that means?"

"No." He glances over at me.

"Simply put, Dallas, you and your brothers are entitled to Calvin Winston's billions. Not to mention the money left to you by your grandfather, who you knew nothing about until now. You and your brothers and honestly, your sister, Danika, stand to become very wealthy individuals—*billionaires,* to be exact.”

Griffyn slams his hands down on the glass surface. “I don’t want that bastard’s money. He lied to our mother, lied to us—I’m glad he’s dead.”

“I don’t know why this is happening. Why now?” I push my chair back and stand. “It’s been years since Calvin Winston died.” As soon as the words leave my mouth, I gasp. “Fuck. Our dad didn’t die in a car accident. He was fucking shot by his son—his *other* son.”

“Good. Piece of shit probably deserved it.” Griffyn stands and moves to the door. “I need a moment.”

Dallas pushes to his feet just as I start to follow our oldest brother out the door. Pausing, I turn to Mr. Abernathy and force a smile.

“Forgive my brothers. If you would, please give us a few moments. This is a lot to take in.”

We get out into the hallway just as Griffyn dips into the men’s room. Dallas glances toward the closed door and sighs. I start to argue, but a soft voice behind me stops my feet from moving.

“So, you’re Ryker.”

Dallas looks past my shoulder. “Let me go talk to him.”

Nodding, I spin and come face to face with a woman dressed to kill. She’s taller than Addison, but the fiery red hair gives her a look I’m certain keeps men’s attention. She cocks her head to the side and smiles.

“I can see why she fell in love with you. Your looks alone would have any woman’s panties melting off.”

"Who are you?" I ignore the *love* remark and arch a brow in silent demand of an answer.

"Libby, Addison's best friend."

"Why isn't she here?"

"I don't know." A strange look passes over her eyes. "I was tied up with a last-minute case and wasn't able to go check on her. She hasn't answered my call, but if her state of mind yesterday is any sign, I'm sure she just couldn't handle coming in today."

Mr. Abernathy chooses that moment to step out of the conference room.

"Mr. Nash, why don't you and your brothers go home and talk things over? Here are both wills for you to read over. We can't do anything about the money from the Winston estate until everyone is here to discuss what happens next. As far as your grandfather's money, we can begin dispersing that as soon as you're ready."

Griffyn and Dallas appear behind him, and I can still see the turmoil written on my eldest brother's face. Dallas shakes his head at me, silently begging me to stay quiet.

"What exactly happens next?" Griffyn's broken voice startles the attorney.

"Well, we'll schedule a meeting with the Winston brothers and the three of you, then discuss how to move forward," Mr. Abernathy explains, glancing back at my brother. "As I explained to Ryker, we can disperse Mr. Dominic's estate immediately."

The truth dawns in Griffyn's eyes, and he snaps his gaze to Dallas, then to me. I can see the fire burning in the cerulean orbs as he stands in a trance. His words dump a bucket of ice on me, and it takes everything inside me not to show how utterly devastated I feel.

"His other children."

"Yes, Griffyn. Your brothers."

Dallas swears as the hall erupts into a flurry of swear words. Libby's wide-eye stare glances between all of us before she shoves her two delicate fingers into her mouth and whistles like she's at the horse races.

"Alright! Enough."

Everyone freezes and stares at the feisty woman.

"I get it. This is a shock to you three, but screaming and yelling isn't going to do a damn thing. I can see why Addison sent the letter instead of just telling you. I can't imagine how you would have reacted to her. Go home… read the will, and I'll call you when *I* get a meeting scheduled." She pivots to walk away, but I grab her arm, stopping her.

"Will you give me Addison's address? She won't return my calls."

"Do you blame her? I know what happened the day she left, Ryker. I wouldn't answer your fucking calls, either."

I take a deep breath and blow it out. "Please… I need to see her."

She silently debates as she holds my gaze.

"I swear to God, if this comes back to bite me in the ass, I'll come to Nashville and cut off your dick."

After pocketing the paper with her address, my brothers and I pile inside the steel cage. The silence confirms their shock runs as deep as mine as the box descends to the ground level. Nobody mentions the news just delivered or the folder clutched in my oldest brother's fingers.

How is it we could go nearly four decades without knowing who we really are?

My thoughts drift to Addison. Is Libby right? Was she afraid to tell me why she was there? *Fuck.* I think back to the times she heard me lose my shit with the two-bit lawyers that constantly hound me. Running my hand over my face, I sigh. My brothers climb into the front of our SUV, but I hesitate.

"You coming, Ryker?" Dallas glances over his shoulder at me.

Nodding my head, I slip into the backseat. "I need to see her."

"Take us to the hotel, then you can use the car to go get your girl." Griffyn turns to me. "But tomorrow, I'll have questions, and she's going to answer them for me."

After dropping them off at the Hilton, I punch the address to her apartments into the GPS. I'm mad, but I don't even know who or what to direct the anger toward. Is it her fault my family is so fucked up? *Probably not.* When I pull up to the curb outside her apartment, I tilt my up at the five-story building and pray she's home.

After parking the SUV, I step out and one thing becomes clear to me. Addison and I are completely different, but I can't help remembering the way she calms the darkness inside me. With everything spinning out of control and everything out of my grasp, she's the only thing that felt real. Not once did she seem infatuated with my former life. She looks past the 'Saint' and sees me—Ryker. Even if I'm not sure who *I* am right now, I know she doesn't care. Despite the lies she told to protect me—and probably herself—I'm in love with her.

This time she isn't going to hide from the truth…. Addison is *mine* and I'm not giving up.

And anyone who knows me, knows the 'Saint' *never* loses a fight.

20

Addison

I'M IN HELL, that's what I think as I lift my head and light assaults my vision. The pounding in my head beats against my skull like the drummer of Nirvana hashing out a set. Blinking through the pain, two things become painfully obvious. One, I'm in my apartment with my hands tied in front of me sitting in a chair... and two, I'm not alone. The memory washes over me like a busted water pipe as the burning ache at the back of my skull throbs where Mr. Uninvited hit me with his gun.

Speaking of Mr. Uninvited, he leans against the counter, staring at me with a look of pure evil, making me shudder.

"You're finally awake."

The thick Russian accent washes over me, and I'm hit with something familiar. It suddenly hits me why. I recognize him as one of the guys standing beside the SUV Andrei got into.

"Why am I tied up?"

"Safety precaution." Just as he smiles, the door opens, and Andrei appears like an apparition. "Boss... she's awake."

"I see that." His deep Russian voice holds a hint of irritation as he stands in front of me. "Miss Quincy, we meet again."

His words from our last encounter filter through my mind *'Take care, Addison. You never know where evil lurks.'* He was referring to himself that day. I should have told Ryker about what he said, but I didn't. And now I'm tied up, sitting in a chair at his mercy.

"What do you want with me?"

"Ah… sweet girl. I won't deny desiring your companionship." He steps close and runs a finger down my cheek. "It's not you I want."

I gasp, "Ryker." That's who he wants—why I don't understand. I jerk my face away from his touch. "Then why am I here?"

He steps away from my body and drags a chair out from my table. Sitting down, he pulls up his pants leg and drapes his knee over his other leg. He leans forward with his elbows on his leg.

"Because you're a means to getting what I want."

"Well, I hate to break the news to you, but Ryker doesn't care about me. So, your plan isn't going to get you what you want."

He cocks his head and the slimy grin covering his face causes me to stifle a gag.

"We'll see about that."

A knock at the door causes the goon, who I assume dragged me inside, to jump. He moves to my door and peeks out the peephole.

"Boss." He whispers. "He's here."

"No worries, Bruno." Andrei shifts his chair closer and presses the muzzle of a gun I didn't see before against my head. "Go ahead, open the door. Need I warn you, Miss Quincy, one move and this ends much faster than it needs to?"

Bruno opens the door, and I'm met with Ryker's wide gaze. The shock washes over him quickly as he steps through the door. Ryker makes a move to grab Bruno, but my words bring him back to the present situation—the one where I have a gun to my head.

"Ryker, don't."

"Listen to your woman, Saint. I'd hate for my gun to go off." He digs the metal into my flesh, making me wince. "Sit down. We need to talk."

Ryker jerks out of Bruno's hold, his eyes never straying from mine. "Are you okay?" Concern laces his tone as he drops into a chair near me.

Bruno closes the door, locking it behind him.

Ryker stiffens as Bruno steps forward and pulls his own weapon out to point it at him. The turmoil in Ryker's eyes nearly guts me, and I have to take several deep breaths to quell the vomit rising.

"We seem to be at a turning point in our relationship, Mr. Nash." Andrei drops his leg and grabs my hair. "You see, my boss needs something from you… and you now need something from me."

I cry out when he jerks my head to the side. Ryker flinches, his hands balling into fists at his sides. His throat bobs as he swallows, his eyes flicking between Andrei's grasp on my hair and my face.

"The way I see it, you either do what I want… or she dies."

I whimper at his statement, fear clawing at me from the inside out.

"You can't get away with this," Ryker growls.

"I can do *whatever* I want, Mr. Nash. Mr. Lipovsky's reach extends beyond Phoenix and is well past the confines of the law. Even here in Atlanta, he has people on his payroll who can make things *disappear.*"

"Why does he want me? What happened to Ivan Gurin was an accident, but had he fought fair, he wouldn't be dead. He got too cocky, and one fucking hit changed his life and mine."

"True… he didn't abide by the rules set by our boss and got himself killed. But now our organization is down a special lackey. One who could make things happen when we needed it."

I realize now this man wants Ryker to become his hired muscle. One he can hide behind the lights and glory of fame. Something I'm sure the boxer they're talking about did.

"You want me to sully my hands for him?" Ryker speaks with disgust as he continues to watch me for any signs of discomfort. "Can't you find someone else? Someone with no morals?"

"This is what you owe Mr. Lipovsky." Andrei stands, his hand dropping the strands of hair he was holding me by. "Think it over, Ryker. You either do what we ask, or I'll find her, and she will disappear. And I promise, she'll wish for death. A woman as beautiful as her would bring a mighty fine price." He jerks me to my feet and presses the gun to my head again.

"What do you want me to do?" Ryker's voice cracks as Andrei moves us toward the door. "I'll do it… whatever you want, if you'll leave her alone."

"Ryker." I whimper his name, not liking what he's about to do..

He pins me with a look that cracks my soul in two. "I have to… I can't lose you."

A hiccup of a sob rips out of me, and the hot tears trickle down my face as Andrei stops at the door.

"You're going to fight at the Knockout in Vegas in two months."

"Why? What do you get if I do?"

Andrei nods toward Bruno to open the door, ignoring Ryker's question.

"Yes or no, Mr. Nash? I haven't got all day."

"Ryker." I finally find my voice, and this time, I practically beg him. "Don't do this… I'm not worth this."

"You're worth everything, Princess." He holds my gaze, before sliding his eyes to Andrei. "Fine. I'll do it. But after the event, we'll be even. Understand? Once the fight is done and I kill whoever it is you tell me to, this little business relationship will cease to exist."

"You're not in control, Ryker." Andrei grips me, digging his fingers into my shoulder to the point of pain. "Don't try anything when we leave… it won't bode well for you or your family. Mr. Lipovsky will be in touch."

He shoves me forward, and just before I land on my knees, Ryker captures me in his arms. The sound of the door slamming is a distant noise as Ryker envelops me into his arms and lifts me off the ground.

"I got you, Princess." He carries me to the couch where he sits, cradling me against his chest. "I'm going to cut this off your wrists, baby."

Nodding, because again I'm incapable of speaking, I watch as he digs out a pocketknife from his pants and cuts through the scratchy bind holding my hands together. Ryker reaches for the glass of water left over from last night and thrusts it at me.

"Drink this, sweetheart."

Tears fill my eyes as the reality of what's happening hits me. Ryker wipes a stray tear that breaks loose and dribbles down onto my skin with the pad of his thumb.

My voice is barely a whisper. "We need to call the cops."

"You heard him." Ryker's deep voice rumbles in his chest, jolting my senses. "He has people in his pocket. We can't take the chance of him finding out and taking you, Princess. He threatened to fucking sell you... *sell you.*" He tightens his arms around me. "I won't risk it."

It suddenly dawns on me that he is here, in my apartment.

"Why are you here?"

"I came to apologize, Princess. I was wrong about what I did to you, and I've been barely holding on to my sanity with the thought that I might have hurt you."

Sighing in frustration, I squash my desire to notify the cops.

"As much as I hate it, you're probably right in thinking the cops might not be helpful. But you should call your brothers. Maybe they can talk some sense into you." I stiffen in Rykers' embrace, realizing why he's likely in Atlanta. "You're here because of the letter."

"Yes, Addison. We came to talk to you about that, and... well, I came for *you.* And while I didn't handle the news well, my brothers thought it was wise to come here and clear things up. Plus, I talked to your friend, Libby. She enlightened me on some things."

"Libby did?" I search his face for the truth. "And did she help you clear things up?"

"Look. We aren't calling the cops, and I'm not telling my brothers. The fewer people involved, the better. But I do need to call Luke and let him know what's going on. He's my partner at the gym and will wonder why I've suddenly come out of retirement." He blows out a breath. "And yes, your friend helped me get my head on straight. She's pretty scary."

"Yeah, that sounds like Libby." Ryker clenches his arms at my agreement. "When are you going back to Nashville?"

"Griffyn and Dallas are back at the hotel reading over the will. Tomorrow, we have a meeting with the Winstons, then we'll go from there."

"You're going to meet with them?"

"I need to know, Addison." Ryker sighs, his warm breath heating my skin. "Did they know we existed, or were they in the dark their whole lives, too?"

"I don't think they knew. I sent them a letter as well—no one had reached out to them before that, as far as I know."

"You did?" Ryker shifts me in his lap and cups my cheek. "Why didn't you just tell me, Addison? Do you even care about me?"

Closing my eyes, I lean into his touch, craving the closeness it gives me.

"The only thing that wasn't real was me needing a job. But me staying in Nashville had nothing to do with your case, Ryker."

"What did it have to do with Addison?"

"It had to do with falling in love with you and not being able to figure out how to tell you the truth without losing you." A tear dripped onto his skin. "Funny enough... I lost you, anyway."

21

Ryker

TURNING her body so she's straddling me, I cup her cheeks with my hands.

"You didn't lose me, Addison. I came for you… for *us*. If there can be an *us*, that is. I fucked up—majorly. All I can see when I close my eyes now is the look of devastation on your face when you scrambled off the floor and ran out of my office. I'm ashamed of myself for the man I became in that moment."

Hot liquid flows down her face as she digests my words. I can see her mind working overtime, and all I want to do is lean forward and press my lips against hers. But I owe her this first. She deserves so much more than what I feel like I can give her, but I want her, anyway.

"I shouldn't have gone into your office. Luke warned me, but the guilt I was carrying decided for me. And part of me feels like I deserved what happened."

"Deserved it?" I lace my fingers into her hair and pull her forehead against mine. "No one deserves what I did, Princess. If I could take it back, I would. You deserve to be treasured, not demoralized.

Never, ever, take the blame for something someone else does wrong… me included." Her eyelashes brush against my skin, the feather touch sending sparks through my veins. "I'm here, begging you to forgive me, Addison. I've never felt this way for a woman… never wanted a woman like I want you. But I've got baggage and darkness that surrounds me. I'm afraid of tainting your light."

"My light?" She leans back, severing the connection between us. "I lied to you, Ryker. How can you possibly believe I'm a good person? I wish I could go back, too, and start all over. I'd tell you from the start why I showed up at your gym. And maybe that would mean not having you like I did, but at least you wouldn't be sitting here hurting from my callous decision."

Addison tries to stand, but I tighten my hold on her hair, keeping her planted on my lap. "I'm not mad about that anymore. I get it, Addison. I would've lied if I was in your shoes, too. If you can look me in the eye and tell me that everything that happened between us was a lie as well, I'll get up and walk out that door. But I know what I felt when we were together, Princess."

"Ryker." She whimpers my name, the tears glistening on her skin. "You said it before… we're like fire and gasoline."

Cupping her cheek, I brush my thumb across the pinkened flesh.

"Then burn with me, baby, and let our flames be the light in our darkness."

I hold my breath, praying she'll be mine. I don't deserve it, but I want it more than I want my next breath. Even if she walks away, I'll protect her with my life. Giving in to Andrei is an easy choice if it means keeping her out of his clutches.

Addison presses her palm against my cheek. Her eyes search my own, but the whisper of her voice nearly does me in.

"I don't want to be in the dark anymore."

She leans forward and presses her lips against mine, a move I'm not prepared for. I take two-point-three seconds to snap out of my shock and take over the kiss. What started as a tender reconnect between two halves of a whole becomes something bordering illicit. Pushing off the couch, I lift her body at the same time, cupping her ass as I do.

"Tell me you want this," I mumble against her lips. "Tell me you're mine."

"I'm yours, Ryker."

In a swift movement, I hurry with her in my arms toward her bedroom. I've barely stepped foot into her room before she's tearing at the button-up shirt I'm wearing. Frustration takes over, and she rips it open, sending buttons across the floor. Her nails scrape against my chest, sending a tiny tendril of electricity straight to my cock.

"Fuck, Princess."

I toss her onto the mattress and pull the material all the way off. Fumbling with my belt, I get it open and unsnap my pants. Shoving them down, along with my underwear, I nearly fall trying to kick off my shoes in order to remove all my clothes. Addison is stripping off her own clothes, but I climb between her legs and stop her from peeling the cotton bra and thong off herself.

"Let me."

Addison props up on her elbows, her eyes watching me as I pop the clasp between her tits and ease the covering away. She lifts one arm at a time, letting me completely divest her body from the bra. Throwing it over my shoulder, I move to the thin cotton thong covering the curls on her mound. The white material is translucent with her desire, and I can't stop myself from rubbing my thumb across the wetness.

"You're soaking, Princess. Is this for me?" I slip a finger beneath the elastic and dip it into her warm center. "Fuck, Addison."

Palming her breast, I roll her nipple between my fingers as the other hand explores her folds. She clenches her pussy as a moan escapes her lips, making my dick pulse against her leg. Her eyes snap open and immediately lower to my shaft. Licking her lips at the sight of pre-cum dripping from the tip, her breaths come out faster. Releasing her nipple, I grasp my shaft and drag my hand along the length.

"You want this, baby? You want my cock inside your sweet little pussy?" I continue fingering her, loving how her body responds to my dirty words. "You like that, don't you, Princess? The dirty talk?"

She whimpers, her hips bucking into my ministration to her swollen nub.

"That's it, Addison. Ride my fingers. Coat them in that sweet cream of yours so I can lick them clean."

Her eyes pinch closed as her body tightens into a coil, then snaps when I curve my finger inside her. Hitting that fleshy spot inside her womb detonates her orgasm, and she screams out, her pussy pulsating around my hand. The rush of liquid that comes out coats my hand.

"Fuck, baby. You squirted all over my hand." I withdraw my fingers, looping them around the thin material and shredding them from her body. "Need a taste," I mumble, slurping the remnants off my digits.

Shifting my weight, I press my face between her legs and suck the soft flesh into my mouth. The sweet musk covering her labia nearly makes me cum, but I ignore the burn in my balls and devour her like a man starved.

"Oh my God, Ryker." Her legs tighten around my head, and for a brief second, I think she might smother me. "I'm going to cum again."

And boy, does she. If this is how I meet my maker, I'll die a happy man. Because fuck, her essence coats my tongue, and I swear I hear angels singing. Once she stops pulsing against my mouth and I've completely licked her clean, I kiss my way up her body and cover her lips with mine. Addison moans against me, no doubt tasting herself on them.

When she wraps her legs around my hips, my dick presses against her opening. Easing my hand between us, I guide myself into her waiting channel and groan when I seat myself completely.

"Fuck, Princess, you feel so fucking good." Pushing up on my palms, I glance down at where our bodies are joined. Seeing my cock slide in and out of her body is the most erotic thing I've ever seen, or so I thought. But Addison shocks the shit out of me as she slips her hand between us and swirls her finger across her clit. The sight alone makes me want to shoot my load inside her, but I'm not ready. Not yet.

"Ryker... please. I need..." She arches her back.

"What do you need, baby?" I thrust into her, enthralled by the way her body moves beneath me.

"Harder... I'm so close again."

Shifting my weight, I lift her leg to my shoulder as I lean onto my knees. My hands cup her breasts, pinching and kneading the perfect handful. Her body bends as her eyes close, but I need to see her sparkling eyes on me as she unravels.

"Open your eyes, Princess. Let me see you… watch me as I fill this sweet pussy with my seed." I pound into her, my fingers slipping to her hips and grasping hold for leverage. "I'm going to coat the inside of, marking you as mine, Princess. You ready, baby? You ready to be mine completely?"

"Ryker." She moans my name, her gaze locking with mine. "Fill me. Make me yours."

With those words, her walls spasm around my shaft. Our eyes stay locked, as if caught in a swirling vortex taking us to heaven. I lengthen inside her, then with a force I never knew possible, I explode deep inside her. Cum jets out of me, painting her womb with my sperm. My body jerks with intensity and swear I've transcended to another universe. When I finally float back down from paradise, Addison is watching me with a look that stills my breathing. Her deep green orbs glisten with emotion that threatens to pull me under.

"What's wrong, Addison? Did I hurt you?" I pull out and start to move away, but she stops me by laying her hand on my forearm.

Her finger traces in circles along my skin, as a smile, bright like the sun, covers her face.

"I love you, Ryker."

A sob tears from my soul, and I collapse against her, pulling her frame into my hold. I'm not ashamed to cry in front of her, because damn, her words undo me in the best way.

"I don't deserve your love, but I'm too selfish not to take it." I roll her body toward me. "I love you too, Princess."

"We should shower." She drags her nails across my chest. "Then go talk to your brothers."

"I don't want to think about my brothers when I have you naked in bed, Princess. But you're right. We need to shower."

I roll off the bed, pulling her with me. Scooping her into my arms, I carry her naked frame into her bathroom. Once I get the water on, we step beneath the heated rainfall. Soaping my hands, I run them over her perfect body, paying extra attention to the parts that make her moan. When the water finally runs cold, and I've shown her exactly how I plan to worship her for as long as she'll let me, we emerge from the stall.

Our lovemaking doesn't stop there. We spend the rest of the night exploring each other in ways I've never experienced with another woman. Finally, exhausted from the uncharted navigation of our bodies, we fall into a perfect slumber. Thoughts of Aleski Lipovsky, his goon, Andrei, or the Winston brothers fall away, and the only thing that matters is *us*.

Tomorrow will bring pain and anger, but for now, I'll give myself to Addison and keep the monsters that terrorize me away. Lies and secrets brought us together, then nearly tore us apart. But what doesn't kill us will make us stronger, right?

And I know without doubt I'm stronger with her... and *nothing* will tear us apart again.

22

Addison

WAKING up in Ryker's arms felt right. His embrace made me feel like nothing could knock us off our cloud of bliss.

Until this very moment.

Sitting across from his brother's penetrating glares makes me shift nervously in the chair beside him. After we peeled ourselves out of bed, he called and asked them to meet us at my place. It didn't take them long to arrive. Now, I'm sitting here, waiting for their pissed-off glares to fade and one of them to talk—it's like being walked to the executioner's chair.

"So you felt like we needed to know what was going on and concocted this farce that you needed a job? Am I getting this right so far?" Griffyn narrows his gaze on me, and I swallow down the nerves threatening to come out as vomit.

"Partially, yes." I wiggle, bumping my leg into Ryker, who presses his palm against the knee, vibrating like a jackrabbit. Glancing over at him, he gives me a reassuring smile. "I came to deliver the information in person, but when I walked into the gym, everyone was busy doing something. The phone started ringing, and no one was making a move to get it, so I answered it."

Dallas erupts into a fit of laughter. "You answered the phone?" He shakes his head. "You've got balls, I'll give you that."

"Well…" I clear my throat. "He thought I was there for the want ad and offered me the job on the spot. I realize now, it might have been slightly stupid to take him up on the offer, but here we are. I didn't mean to hurt him, or you two, but it frustrated me that my boss didn't feel the same urgency I did. Of course, I didn't know about the letter or the revelation about your father. All I knew was you were entitled to a shitload of money. The kind of money that's life changing."

"And what do you get out of it, Addison?" Griffyn leans forward, waiting for my reply.

Confusion hits me. "I don't understand what you mean."

"Is there something you gain from telling us about the money?"

Ah, I see. He thinks I wanted to ask them for some sort of compensation.

"Nothing, Griffyn. I gain nothing in telling you—at least not money, like you're thinking. I wanted to make partner with Abernathy & Fitzgerald. That's why I did it. My boss told me if I could get you, any of you, to come to Atlanta, he'd give me the promotion."

"Wait, you said *wanted*, as in *past* tense." Dallas catches the slip.

Looking over at Ryker, I smile. "Something else is more important. I tendered my resignation this morning."

"You did what?" Ryker digs his fingers into my knee. "You didn't say anything to me."

Shit, did I not read him right last night? I thought he and I were going to explore our relationship, and I can't do that from here when he's in Nashville. Seeing the panic on my face, he reaches out and cups my cheek.

"Hey, take a breath."

Sucking in air, I blink back my stupid tears.

"I thought you'd be happy. If we're going to do this,"—I waggle my finger between our bodies—"being in Atlanta when you're in Nashville will make it impossible."

"I could've moved here for you."

"No, Ryker, you couldn't," I disagree, shaking my head. "Your family is there. You own a business, and now that you're going to box again, I need to be the one to move to you."

"Wait... box again? What's she talking about?" Griffyn interrupts.

I cringe realizing my mistake. "Shit, Ryker. I'm sorry."

"No, it's okay, Addison. They would have learned about it, eventually." He turns to his siblings. "I've agreed to fight in the Knockout Match in Vegas in two months."

"Why?" Dallas folds his arms across his chest. "You've refused for a year... why all the sudden?"

"I'm doing it for Axel. He's new to the sport and asked me to come with him." The lie rolls off his tongue, and I wince at putting him in the position of lying to his brothers.

Griffyn narrows his gaze on his brother. "I feel like there's something you're not telling us."

Ryker pulls me against him and blows out a breath. "Well, I figured why not. Plus, while we're in Vegas, Addison and I are getting married."

"What?" Dallas and I say at the same time.

Ryker turns my body to face him. Brushing a stray lock of hair from my face he grins.

"I love you, Addison. And when I find something I love, I don't let it go—therefore I'm not letting you go. Marry me, Princess. Say you'll be mine in every sense of the word."

My heart pounds against my chest as the blood rushes in my ears. Closing my eyes, I let my feelings surface, and all I feel is completeness. It may be fast, but this man has captured my heart and soul completely. Opening my lids, I find Ryker's cobalt gaze filled with fear—and hope. A slow smile creeps out, and I nod my head, whispering my answer.

"Yes… I'll marry you, Ryker. *You.* Not the 'Saint,' not the money you're about to inherit. I'll marry Ryker Nash, the man whose shown me who the man beneath the mask he wears really is." My lips cover his, showing him how much he means to me.

"Well, shit, are we still Nash?" Dallas' words cut through the moment, and I can't help but giggle.

"Really, Dallas?" Ryker growls. "I ask my woman to marry me, and you fuck it up with a stupid question like that. Of course we're still a Nash. Bryson adopted us, remember?"

This time it's Griffyn who speaks. "But was it legal?"

"Fuck." Ryker rubs the bridge of his nose in frustration. "I don't know, okay?"

I elbow him on the side playfully. "I don't care what your last name is, Ryker. It doesn't change the fact I love you."

"Good." He slips out from beneath me and holds his hand out. "Because there is no telling how this meeting is going to go. Let's get it over with so we can go home."

I let him pull me up and together, with his brothers, we head down to the SUV. The air is thick with tension as we drive to my former place of employment, knowing their lives are going to be different when they walk out. For some reason, I can't shake the feeling that this mess is just the tip of the iceberg. Of course, Ryker and I have other problems to deal with, but I'll keep my promise to keep it quiet, even if I think it's wrong to keep it from his brothers.

Libby immediately rushes forward and pulls me into an embrace. "You're quitting?" She whispers into my ear, disbelief in her pitch.

"Yes. I'm going to Nashville." I lean back and smile at my best friend. "He asked me to marry him."

"What?" she squeals. "Fuck this. I'm coming, too."

"What?"

"I hate this place, Addison. Being here without you is going to be a nightmare. I don't have to work, you know that." Libby is a trust fund baby, but always insisted on working, although she's a millionaire. "I'll find a place to stay, then worry about work."

"Okay, then. Well, let's get this shit over with so we can pack." Turning to Ryker, I say, "Libby is moving to Nashville."

He smiles. "I'm glad, baby. You deserve to have your friend close by."

Holding his hand, I lead him down the hall into the conference room. Ryker pulls out a chair for me, then takes the one beside me. Mr. Abernathy steps into the room and sits at the head of the table.

"Mr. Winston will be here shortly. Unfortunately, his brothers could not attend today, but he assures me once he knows this is legit, he will bring them all later."

"Are you nervous?" I whisper softly into his ear, trying to gauge where his head is at.

He shrugs. "Not nervous per se, but on edge, if that makes sense."

I'm about to reply when the sound of the door opening interrupts me. Turning my head, I watch as a man with hair a shade darker than Ryker's steps into the room. He's dressed in an Armani suit and has an air of danger around him. A blonde woman holds onto his arm, almost like she's his anchor in a turbulent sea. He guides her around the table, and I watch as my former boss rises and holds out his hand.

"Mr. Winston, thank you for joining us."

Ryker tenses beside me, and I struggle not to pull him against me, to comfort him. Instead, I lace my fingers with his and squeeze. The room is stale with unspoken questions. I can't help but notice how Mr. Winston scans the room, pausing on Griffyn. There's something in his gaze that makes my throat tighten with emotion, but I shake it off, not wanting to cause additional issues for Ryker. Catching my stare, Mr. Winston blinks away whatever held him hostage on the oldest brother and turns to face the rest of us.

"Mr. Nash," Mr. Abernathy looks at Griffyn. "Since you're the eldest sibling, I'd like to address you first. This is Drake Winston and his fiancée, Rhiannon."

Drake Winston is silent as they have a silent stare off again and the thick tension between them makes me shift uncomfortably in my seat. Finally, his deep voice fills the room.

"This comes as a shock to me, as it will to my brothers."

"You haven't told them?" Ryker speaks, causing Drake's eyes to shift to him.

"No," he answers, shaking his head. "We've been dealing with my brother Gage's injuries sustained from a car accident. He's been in the hospital for two weeks, and I didn't want to bring this to him until I was sure of the legitimacy of the letter. My youngest brother and his wife just welcomed triplets into the world. I just needed to be *certain*." His voice is barely a whisper on the last word, but it's clear he doesn't question things after seeing them in person. Even I can see the resemblance in the man sitting across from me and the one I love.

"Certain about what? That we weren't running a scam on you?"

He starts to speak, but his fiancée, Rhiannon, presses her hand to his arm.

"We don't think you're scamming us, Mr. Nash. Drake is well aware of what his father is capable of, but he needed to see with his own eyes that this was real."

"I'm sorry." Ryker acquiesces, shaking his own head. "It was a shock to us as well. Our whole lives we thought our father was Seth Winter, a man who died in a car accident when we were still kids. To find out it was all a lie… well, we're on edge ourselves."

"What do you need to prove we are who that letter says?" Dallas pipes up from beside me. "DNA? Because I can tell you I don't want your money or *his*. I want nothing to do with his blood money."

Drake suddenly smiles. "I don't need DNA to know it's true. And I didn't want his money either, but I took it and turned it into something just to spite him. You could do the same..." He pauses.

"Dallas. My name is Dallas, and this is Ryker. Our sister, Danika, is still in Nashville."

"Yes, Ryker Nash, the famous 'Saint.' I believe you met my brother in prison. Do you remember him?"

"'Fraid not. I was out of it when he saved my life. And when I got out, I wanted to bury what happened in the past, so I never reached out. I regret that now."

Griffyn pushes to his feet. "I can't do this. I need a minute."

We watch as he storms from the room. Ryker moves to stand, but I stop him.

"Let me. You finish here while I see to him."

Kissing him on the cheek, I hurry from the room in search of his brother. It doesn't take me long to find Griffyn tucked away in Libby's office. She gives me a sympathetic look as she steps out and leaves us alone.

"Hey, you okay?" I move into the office and sit in front of him.

"No." His eyes are glossed over as he meets my gaze. "How could I not know? I should have seen something... noticed something."

"Griffyn, that's not reasonable to think." I press my hand to his knee. "You were just a child. It wasn't your responsibility to know these things. I know this is hard, but look on the bright side." He furrows his brow in confusion. "Your family just got bigger. I'd give anything to have a big family, but it's just me now. Stop looking at this as a burden and see it for what it can be. You have three men who are very well your brothers. I know that's a shock, but it can't get any worse. Only better, right?"

"I wish I had your faith, Addison. I can see why my brother fell in love with you. I hope you're right, but I can't shake this foreboding feeling. Look, I don't know what more we can do today. Will you tell my brothers I took an Uber back to the hotel? I just need some time alone, and I want to call my sister. She's about to get money she knows nothing about."

"Of course, Griffyn."

He stands and pulls me into a hug. "And Addison?" He moves away from me, a small smile playing on his lips. "You're not alone anymore, and if you're right, you just got three new brothers as well."

With that, I watch as Griffyn steps into the elevator. Libby glances my way and smiles.

"I take it didn't go well?"

"I don't know about that…" I shrug, not sure how to respond. "It's a lot to digest. I just hope this is the only thing to come out of this. I don't think Griffyn will handle any more surprises."

I turn on my heel and head back to the conference room. No matter what happens, I'll stand by Ryker and his family, because Griffyn was right—I'm not alone anymore.

23

Ryker

"I'M SORRY ABOUT THAT." I watch as Dallas exits the building. He's just as shaken as Griffyn and needed a moment to compose himself. "Hopefully, this will all settle down, and we can move forward. When do you think you'll tell your brothers about us?"

Drake pauses, mulling over my question. "I'd like Gage to be well enough to handle the shock. Finding out we have half-siblings is going to rock our family. But that's going to be the easiest thing for him."

"What do you mean?" I pull Addison against me, needing her warmth.

Rhiannon gives Drake a weird look, then shakes her head no. Drake smiles at her, pulling her to him. He places a kiss on her forehead and tucks her against his side.

"When Gage sees all of you, there will be no doubt you're our family."

Feeling like there is a cryptic message in his words, I bristle. "What aren't you telling me?"

Drake turns toward me with an expression that shakes me to my core. Whatever he's about to share isn't something good. Sensing my tension, Addison wraps her arm around my side.

"Let's just say, while I believe you and Dallas are my half-brothers, I don't feel the same about Griffyn."

"What the fuck?" I take a step forward, but Addison tightens her hold. "Why would you say that?"

He shakes his head. "Let's just say seeing is believing. And if I had to guess, Griffyn is more than half."

"I don't understand. You're telling me something, but I'm being daft here—you think Griffyn is your full brother? Which would make him mine and Dallas' *half*-brother?"

Drake simply shrugs and starts to walk away, but I call out to him.

"Wait… you can't just say that and not answer me."

He stops, glances over his shoulder, and smirks. "Ryker, seeing is believing. My brother has been in the news a lot lately. Take a few days… look us up. Once you do,"—he pulls out a card and hands it to me—"call me. We'll go from there on figuring out how to control this fucked-up situation. Until then, that's all you'll get from me. I'm going to dig into the past and unravel the lies that are so blatant, it's comical."

Addison and I watch as he exits the building with his fiancée by his side.

Sliding my phone out, I pull out of Addison's hold and step to the side. Quickly opening a browser, I type in Gage Winston. My phone seems to take on a turtle's pace as the page loads. Multiple links fill the screen with new articles about his recent car accident.

Clicking the first link, I read the story.

Doctor Gage Winston was rushed to the emergency room after being t-boned in the intersection of Howell Mill and 17th Street by a driver under the influence. Dr. Winston was taken to surgery upon arrival to repair a leg fracture.

The other driver was pronounced dead at the scene.

"What did you find?" Addison props her chin on my shoulder, peering down as I scroll through the article. "Oh my God."

Her words are like lead in my chest as my finger stops on the photo attached to the article.

"*Fuck.*"

I enlarge the screen, and fear ices through my veins when I come face to face with Drake's hidden message. There, staring back at me is my brother. Only it's *not* my brother. A pair of unique blue eyes, identical to Griffyn's stare back—only these eyes belong to Gage Winston.

"How is this possible?"

Addison wraps her arms around me. "I don't know, but we'll figure it out together. But Ryker?"

"Yeah?"

"We can't tell Griffyn until we know what the hell is going on."

Addison has my full attention now. "Why would you suggest keeping this from him?"

"He was so broken when he left the office. He felt like something more was going to happen, and he didn't know if he could deal with it. So, for now, I think we keep this between the three of us. Until we know the *how*. Besides, we still have the other issue to deal with."

She's right. Dealing with this drama made me forget about my own mess. I don't know how I'm going to keep two secrets from my family. The weight of it is already bringing me down.

"I need to call my uncle. He has to know something."

I notice Dallas staring at us. "Ryker." His voice cracks as he comes closer. "I was curious about our new family."

Fuck. That means he did exactly what I did and Googled them. My thoughts immediately went to Griffyn, and I worry about him doing the same.

"You know."

"How is this possible?"

"I don't know, Dallas, but I know who might."

"Uncle Dominic." He nods in agreement. "Well, how about we go pay him a visit before heading home to Nashville?"

"I was going to just call him, but I like your idea better. Addison, prepare yourself. We're going to visit my uncle at work."

"Okay..." Confused, she glances between Dallas and me. "Is that a bad thing?"

"Depends on how you feel about sex clubs."

Dallas

Sitting across from my Uncle Dominic and his new wife, Sabrina, it takes everything in me not to make a scene. But this is my livelihood as well, so I keep my mouth shut and listen. Glancing over at Addison, Ryker's fiancée, I can't help the giggle that bubbles up. She's gripping Ryker's arm like someone's going to kidnap her and do unspeakable things to her. Her eyes are frozen to the monitors mounted on the walls.

While the club doesn't have cameras in the private rooms, they are scattered throughout the common areas, giving her an up-close private viewing of the activities in Vibe. Pulling my attention back to the conversation, I startle.

"I'm sorry. Did you say something to me?" I ask, glancing at the faces staring at me.

Dominic shrugs. "I asked if you could forgive me?"

My mind races with everything he told us, and I blanch at his question.

"I'm not sure. I don't understand how you could let my mother believe the lies—all of them." Guilt radiates off him.

"I made a mistake, Dallas. One I've lived with my entire adult life. I'm not asking you to understand why I did it. I'm asking you to forgive me. I fucked up. I can't take it back, nor can I change things now. I didn't realize what kind of man Calvin Winston was, but I learned quickly. I've been fighting to keep the trash he associated with out of my club since giving in to his blackmail. So, don't think for a minute I've had it easy."

"What about your sister?" Ryker tightens his hold on Addison's hand. "My mother loved you. You were her brother, and she trusted you—you let her die thinking her son was dead."

"She knew." His words are like an arrow to my heart.

"What the fuck did you just say?"

"Your mother knew. She found out not long after Calvin died, but she and Byron felt it was best to keep the secret—even if it nearly killed her. Though I suspect our grandfather played a role in that as well."

"I can't do this." Ryker stands, pulling Addison to her feet. "I'm sorry, Uncle Dominic. I know you're the only family left of Mom, but this... this is too much. Dallas, we're leaving." He turns to Sabrina. "It was nice to meet you. I wish it was under better circumstances."

Addison smiles at the woman. "Congratulations on your pregnancy." She follows my brother out, clutching his hand like she knows he needs the physical touch to ground him.

Bringing my eyes back to my uncle, I don't miss the utter devastation in his eyes as he watches my younger brother leave, knowing it might be the last time he sees him. Unfortunately, I'm tied to him through the club in Nashville as part owner.

"What do I need to do?" He looks over at me, tears glistening in his gaze. "How can I fix it?"

"You can't. Not right now. Maybe in time, we'll get past this, but Loren…" Using his first name causes him to stiffen. "You fucked up in a way I'm not sure is salvageable. And if it weren't for the fact that I own half of Vibe in Nashville, I'd be walking out of that door, too. But I can't because it's all I know, and we're short a manager."

I watch as he relaxes and grins. "Actually, I owed someone a favor, so I hired an acquaintance of theirs."

"I know you own part of the club, but if you care about me at all, you'll avoid me for a bit. Once this guy shows up, you can communicate with him about club business." As if hiring someone will fix what he's done. "We're leaving in the morning and won't be back until Drake calls us."

He deflates again as I push to my feet and move toward the door.

"I understand." He stands, tucking his wife into his side. "I'm sorry, Dallas. For everything."

Giving him a nod, I step to the door and pause. "What's the guy's name you're sending?"

"Will."

"Nice to meet you, Sabrina," I say, dipping my chin at his wife.

I find Ryker and Addison waiting by the SUV when I step outside. She's buried in his hold, and as I draw closer, I can see she's whispering something in his ear.

"You good?" I tilt my head in question.

"As good as I can be." Ryker opens the door and helps Addison inside. He climbs in beside her and slams the door.

I glance in the rearview mirror at the two of them wrapped in each other's arms.

"I can't believe he knew all this time. This is going to crush Griffyn."

"For now, let's hold off telling him. Let Drake have a chance to tell his brothers and me to get through this upcoming match. Then we can figure out how to navigate the rest."

Part of me wants to say no, but Ryker's right. This secret won't just affect Griffyn—it's going to rock the lives of two families. Shaking my head, I start the car.

"Let's go pack up your house and get your shit loaded in the two cars. The sooner we can get the hell out of this place, the better we'll feel. Shit." I glance back at Ryker again. "We've got to tell Danika something."

"Let's leave out the bit about Griffyn."

I disagree. Our sister is the nosiest person on the planet. It wouldn't surprise me if she already knew something. "You know she's probably already Googled the Winston boys."

"Fuck." He scrubs his hand down his face. "Fine. We'll talk to her alone about it. I hope she can keep this secret. You know how she has loose lips."

As we head toward Addison's, all I can think about is my oldest brother. We're going to learn he's our half-brother or that Gage is Drake's half-brother. Either way, someone... no, make that two someones are going to be devastated.

Pushing everything out of my mind, I wonder about this new guy my uncle hired. I sure as hell pray this favor of his doesn't turn out to be a problem. The last thing I need right now is more drama… and for some reason, I'm getting a bad gut feeling this shit is just scratching the surface.

This guy Will better have his shit together… the last thing I need is for *him* to create more problems for me.

FAMILY SECRETS NEVER STAY SECRET.

At least, that's what Dallas recently learned when the truth about his father came out.

As he grapples with his new reality of being a billionaire, Dallas quickly learns that the 'Winston' name isn't all glitter and gold. Not to mention the new manager Will, his uncle hired for their club, isn't what Dallas expected.

Will is *exactly* the kind of problem he doesn't need or want.

Willow's, aka Will's, snarky attitude and constant defiance make him want to choke her… or worse, turn her over his knee. She thinks he's a billionaire playboy, and Dallas is fine with that perception because it helps him pretend he isn't interested in her long legs or her perfect body of curves.

Though, Dallas realizes it's not *hate* he feels for the woman. But refusing to admit his feelings and the fact he can't handle the maelstrom of trouble his family's facing, Dallas continues to spiral out of control. When trouble becomes bigger than he can manage, he finally accepts help from his newfound brothers.

But it may be too late, and he might lose the one person who can save him from himself... *her*.

Pre-Order Bad Habits and uncover even more secrets because nothing is as it seems in love and family.

Playlist

Scan or click the QR code to listen on Spotify

AVAILABLE

Books

Simply scan or click the QR code for more books

ABOUT

Dori Pulitno

"Welcome to the dark side. We have sexy Mafiosos."

Dori P is the naughtier, much dirtier half of USA Today Bestselling author, LC Taylor. The bad girl Dori embraces her Italian side with heroic hitmen, decadent conflicted dons, and oh so f*ckable assassins trying to trade their devilish ways for salvation and the perfect woman to tie to their bed.

And F**k following the rules… this author is most definitely trigger happy.